Upon a Time in Maine

Wicked Savage Tales

Upon a Time in Maine
Wicked Savage Tales

ISBN: 978-0-9991163-6-4

Library of Congress Control Number: 2021937371

Drawings by John Wilson

Printed in the United States of America

Published by
Free People Publishing
Salem, NH
freepeepub.com

To that little bit of Maineiac in us all

Contents
Ten Stories

Wicked Savage Tale   1
Campers accidentally summon an ancient evil

That Winged Thing   19
Moose Harbor gets a strange, flying guest

Where Did He Go   25
A mysterious hiker comes for a grim harvest

Howlin' Minnie   37
The forest avenges a woman flung from a cliff

Reflections of Mr. Ivy   63
Special vision locates a lingering fiend

When Owen Dropped By   79
The sea sends a fisherman for a final visit

And Then There Were Three   85
Ghost hunters tremble at an abandoned bridge

The Barker and the Pinwheel and That   101
    Game of Karma
Childhood memories twist toward terror

The Return of Mr. Poole   123
Psychotherapy resurrects a small-town tormentor

Prelude to a Storm   153
Two thugs send their victim to a bright reward

Note from the Author   161
Acknowledgments, and how this book came about

"... a howling wilderness does not howl: it is the imagination of the traveler that does the howling."

The Maine Woods, Henry David Thoreau

Deep in the northern forests of Maine lives a monster so vicious that even the natives of that ancient place dare to speak of it only in whispers, and only to warn the innocent: Never invite evil.

Wicked Savage Tale

It would have been funnier if we had had a second or two longer to laugh. If at the very moment I had finished the story, with me and my little theatrics and her still holding the two pieces of fire wood in her hands, we hadn't heard the wood knocks echo through the forest, which was spooky enough. And then came the horrific scream. On cue, as in, as *if*. Wicked savage and ferocious it was. More aptly, I would better describe it as terrifying by the look on Marlene's face. It carried through the ancient forest and bore down on us with the power of a gale force wind. Every hair up and down my arm, on my neck, down my spine, stood on end. If there was any doubt my sphincter was fit to be clamped shut it was then and there. But no! It wavered like a Baptist preacher throwing gospel in an Indiana whore house on a Saturday night.

If you have ever spent time in the Woods of Maine, or any forest for that matter, then you know the sound of any creature in its death throes. The bloodcurdling scream is unmistakable. Yet, there are other sounds, too, that are just as unnerving. Red foxes will let out a wailful

1

screech out of fright or fear. Coyotes will yip and screech and howl, too, to mark their territory and communicate. They will answer each other from the forest's edge to the opposite end of a meadow, or from one side of a wood lot to another. If you've ever been caught between the call of coyotes it's easy to let your imagination and every other part of you run wild. In the ink black darkness of the nighttime forest you begin to wonder if coyotes do attack and if so, is there anywhere at all to run.

For Marlene and me, from where we were in the old forest, I was praying for a shrill cry from another coyote on the opposite side of the forest. At that point, that's what I wanted to hear – coyotes talking to each other – but I knew better. The piercing cry we heard sounded inhumanely human as it drifted off into the ether beyond the other side of no return. A place I was sure we were heading to right then and there. It was out there, that thing of evil, coming our way. What had I done? What had she done? All the stories I had heard about this stretch of forest since I was a child went through my head. Frightening images conjured up in my mind, one after the other. We were in the presence of evil – we had to escape now! Years before, when this happened, it was only a story – that's what I had convinced myself – that none of it was real – that had been my way out then. I looked down the dark trail – the direction from which we had come earlier – the way out now – or was it? The other way was deeper into the forest, darker, into the unknown.

Oh, why did I tell her – the love of my life – that wicked savage tale?

* * *

When I was a kid I'd come up here most summers with my Boy Scout troop. We'd spend a week wandering and hiking through the 100 Mile Wilderness – the most remote part of the Appalachian Trail. We would earn our badges as we made our way deep into the forest. But it was really about the adventure – always a lot of fun. Hiking up and across the spine of the mountains, and climbing up some of the old forest fire lookout towers the Maine Forest Service had erected all across the central and northern part of the state. From the top of the towers we had unobstructed views for hundreds of miles in every direction. But there was more. Coming across a moose knee deep in a pond, a small herd of deer in a meadow, even a black bear that might occasionally cross our path. Once we watched a chain of Canadian lynx walk right through our campsite as if we weren't even there. Curious they were, like house cats. Everyone froze for about five minutes as they sniffed and snooped around, and then meandered off. The best time was sitting around the campfire each evening. After dinner, we'd talk about what we'd accomplished that day, and all that we'd see and do the next. Then, our scoutmaster Mr. Brown, or one of the other parent chaperons, would always have more than one story that would send shivers down our spines. Of all the stories we heard over the course of those summers, my favorite was one about a witch named Howlin' Minnie and the forest she haunted. There were many other good ones, too. All meant to be fun and games ... until that one evening.

We were a day's hike from anywhere, and hadn't passed or encountered another hiker since the late afternoon. We decided to camp near a pond. There was a beaver dam near the outflow, a narrow stream which we fished and caught enough brookies to feed us all that night. Near dusk, the sounds of the forest shifted from day to night. Song birds went to roost and quieted for the night. A bald eagle hovered over its aerie, high atop an ancient birch tree by the edge of the pond, and settled down in its nest of sticks and moss. A pair of owls hooted in turn from somewhere in the forest. Crickets began to chirp. The buzz of mosquitoes and flies was quickly followed by the scent of bug spray, carried by a light breeze that had drifted down from the mountains. The breeze was just enough to rustle the tree tops so we could hear their gentle sway in the dimming light. A thrashing in the woods alerted everyone. To our amazement, a bull moose wandered leisurely from the forest and went knee deep into the pond. Not more than fifty feet from us, we watched its head disappear into the dark water and come up with a mouthful of pondweed. It did so for some time until a whip-poor-will began to sing its lonesome song. The great beast paused as though to listen. What did he hear that we did not? A warning, or simply a signal for him to move on? It shook its head of water, turned and walked leisurely out of the pond and back into the forest.

That turned our attention to dinner and building up the campfire before all light was lost to the stars above. Afterwards, as we did each evening, we sat around the fire and talked of the day behind us and the day ahead – all the while in anticipation of our nightly tale. When the time arrived, Mr. Brown looked over at his friend and our chaperon, Mr. Hall, and said, "Roger, are you ready?" He nodded, and then Mr. Brown began to tell a story like no other one that we'd heard before. He spoke slowly, thoughtfully, like it was all a matter of fact and had really happened. What he told us might have left our imaginations to wonder and wander any other time, on any other occasion, but not that particular night. Looking back, the tale he shared was less for the pleasure of spooking us and more a message. Maybe even a warning, I think, for us all. More along the lines of what the Bard once wrote of, which I would read later in life, that "There are more things in heaven and earth ... than are *dreamt* of..." Mr. Brown seemed to be asking us at the same time as telling us – how is it, in the hierarchy of nature, with the human mind at its pinnacle, that the perception of what is known is such a far cry from what is. And the acceptance of 'what is' is even further than what is known. So began a tale of a forest ranger and the limits of what we really know about the world in which we live.

***

Parker was his name. He'd been a ranger for going on twenty years when they'd sent him to relieve a man at one of the old forest fire lookout tower stations, up past Moosehead Lake on the other side of Misery Gore. Ha! What's in a name! You tell me? Parker knew those woods like the back of his hands. When you're in the Forest Service and you've been there in that district that long, you just don't get lost. He was the guy people turned to when they needed to find their way out. That's why it was such a shocker when he failed to show up. At the checkpoint he had radioed the station that he was half an hour out, maybe less. Later, when the investigation was well under way, Lemieux,

4

the man Parker was supposed to relieve, recalled hearing three loud knocks over the radio while Parker spoke. He thought it odd, even more so, foreboding, but didn't say anything at the time and went back outside to finish splitting wood. Lemieux had Penobscot blood in him. He knew the stories and had been in the forest long enough to know that he would not be walking out that day even when Parker arrived.

The trouble was, Parker never did.

Twenty minutes later there came a burst of static over the radio and an ungodly scream of terror and cry for help. Lemieux called it in immediately, but the office had picked up the scream on its radio too. The sound unnerved the half dozen rangers and office staff who heard it. Poor old Mrs. Robinson, the office secretary, began to fret so badly after the scream she wept openly. Parker was her son-in-law and she loved him dearly. The moment haunted her to such an extent, the trauma of it, that she would have night terrors in the coming months and years ahead. She took to medication, which knocked her out but still left her fitful and restless, and she would still wake up in a cold sweat. The reality was she could never shake it. It never left her until that final day, as her head came to rest upon her pillow for the last time. Even then, her final words spoken on this earthly plane were for him. "The terror," she whispered. "The scream ... oh Parker, what happened to you, my boy?" The truth was she was not alone in suffering night terrors. All the others in the office suffered from them too, at least for a spell.

As for Parker, they found his radio and ranger hat on the trail and nothing else. A frenzied search and rescue went on for days without success. Then quietly, without public announcement, the rescue transitioned into a search and recovery that continued for the rest of the summer. Parker was well-known and well-liked. Some of the best trackers and dogs joined the search parties. They came up from New Hampshire, Vermont, New York, and Pennsylvania. They came down from Ontario and Quebec, and over from New Brunswick and Nova Scotia. Horrible as it was, it was even more mystifying. It was as though he had vanished into thin air ... but for that scream!

5

Lemieux went on leave. He had to ease his pain and sorrow somehow and he chose a month long bender that consisted of Crown Royal and soda, which soon enough morphed to just Crown Royal. He hated himself for not acting and warning Parker when he had heard the knocks. He had never doubted the stories he had heard as a child from his people – the ones on his grandmother's side. She was full blooded and had taken him with her often on visits to the reservation past Old Town. Stories of Pomoola and the Specter Moose had enthralled him, but the stories about the zombie-like creature had terrified him. Malevolent and flesh-eating, an evil spirit – a thing – that devoured body and soul. The warning had been branded in his head as a child's rhyme for forty years:

> Deep in the forest on summer eves,
> Knock three times upon a tree,
> Then prepare for peril that night,
> Of life and limb and boundless fright,
> For if the knocks return in kind,
> The creature comes to seek and find.

Near the end of the search and recovery, after Lemieux had pulled himself out of his ferocious bender, he approached Francis Bear, a lifelong friend of his grandmother and a cultural preservationist for the tribe. While he had trapped, tracked, and hunted the North Woods for most of his life, above all, Bear knew the legends and he knew the creation myths, and knew that not all of those stories were myths at all.

Lemieux told Bear what had happened. For on that fateful day when Parker went missing, while Lemieux was splitting wood outside the station, the head of the maul had come loose. He'd taken one of the pieces of wood he'd split, turned the axe handle upside down and hammered the knob end to drive the handle back through the eye of the axe head – three loud blows that echoed through the forest. Only when he had heard the knocks over Parker's radio did he comprehend what he had done. That's what he feared had really happened to Parker.

"This creature that we seek is known amongst all our people," Bear said to Lemieux, "From Nova Scotia to the Great Lakes. It has many names – the Giwakwa, the Chenoo, and what most know it by these days, the Wendigo. None of these names shall be spoken when we get there lest we alert it to our presence. The monster is thought of as a creature born of winter by nearly all who speak of it in all the creation stories and after. Its heart is frozen through. It thrives in the bitter cold, the long dark nights, and that is when it is most active, when it is most hungry. Yet, in the summer, as the child's rhyme warns, when called, it will rise to feed. It is gluttony and greed, decay and rot, of the soul and mind, and it is contained by no season. Once bitten, the human that once was is no more. The only escape is death ... or this." He held up a glass vile. Lemieux studied the tiny white chunks inside. "Salt distilled from Passamaquoddy Bay and blessed by our brothers there. It will melt the heart of the monster and set all within it free."

On the morning of the 29th of August, Lemieux informed his supervisor, Gordon Hatch, of Bear, his skill set as a tracker and his offer to help. Hatch had never pressed Lemieux about what had happened out there. His remark about the three knocks he had left alone, left to hang there to dry for the past month while Lemieux was on leave. He had heard something similar as a kid himself, as a Boy Scout, around a campfire, about a forest dwelling demon or something, aroused by knocking wood together or against a tree. There wasn't any point to the story at all but to scare the be-Jesus out of the first-time campers and a few older ones who should know better.

"Listen Lemieux, I know you've had a rough time of it," said Hatch, "We all have. I also know of Bear," he added, which was true. He had heard him speak at a symposium in Bangor the previous winter. "He's on the cultural preservation side of things. He's that Francis Bear, correct?"

"Yes, he is," replied Lemieux.

"Good, I respect that, but we need to be clear about a couple of things going into that forest. We all know that the North Woods is unforgiving. Any man, woman, or child could take but a few steps into the forest off the trail – maybe just to relieve themselves – and turn a degree or two in the wrong direction, and rather than walk back to the trail, walk into oblivion. Thirty feet off the trail and you are a blur, forty or fifty feet and you become invisible. Hopelessly friggin' lost – you from the trail and the trail from you. The forest is that dense, that dark."

"I know the forest is unforgiving," said Lemieux, "and so does Bear."

"You're damn right it's unforgiving." Hatch had wondered these past months if something that simple had been Parker's fate. That he went to take a leak and turned the wrong way to go back – walked too far in the wrong direction. Maybe now he's laying there, what's left of him, seventy feet off the trail. Could that possibly be it? … And then he remembered the scream.

"I appreciate Bear's help and it's welcome," said Hatch.

"Thank you," said Lemieux. "We'll get on it tomorrow."

"Yes, we will," replied Hatch. The remark took Lemieux by surprise. Hatch could see it in his eyes. "Dorsey out of Augusta is coming up in the early afternoon. He's working on Parker's file, said he needs to follow up on a few things. He's by the book and will want to tag along. I have no idea if he's ever heard of Francis Bear and I'm not going to ask him."

"The four of us, then," said Lemieux.

"Tomorrow at 3 p.m. we'll head out for the station," Hatch nodded. "We may have to spend the night."

On the afternoon of the 30th of August, after brief introductions, the four men entered Misery Gore. They followed the trail deep into the forest toward the tower station, following the footsteps of Parker, they reasoned. The trail through the wilderness was winding, twisted, and rugged. It went directly over, beside, and around moss covered boulders, some bigger than dump trucks, with wild blueberry bushes and stunted cedar growing atop them. They weaved their way through thick spruce and hemlock groves, carefully and constantly avoiding rocks and exposed roots where they stepped. The trail rose up, steeply in places, and then leveled off for a while. It wound past ponds, over brooks and streams, and continued to rise. After several hours they came upon the spot where Parker lost his radio and contact with this world. When the men came to a stop, Lemieux realized Parker had been closer to the station than he remembered. It filled him with fear, but also regret.

Dorsey looked around. "This is it – the place?" he asked. He was sweating profusely, more than the other men. Desk life can do that to you.

"This is the place," Hatch replied. "Rough hike, but the trail is well marked."

"Good thing we brought the tracker along." Dorsey threw a thumb in Bear's direction and grinned, but no one else did. "Yes, well, I can see how a man could lose his bearings up here," Dorsey corrected himself. "And you sure as hell need to be in shape." He offered a faint smile, and, to change the subject, asked, "How far to the station?"

"Just ahead," Lemieux answered, "a few more minutes."

"We did three-hundred sixty degrees from this point," said Hatch with a sweep of his hand. "Our radius went out for miles – even though you saw what we went through – we went through it looking for him."

"Has anyone bothered to dig straight down?" Dorsey smiled a silly grin. "With his hat and radio left behind, maybe the earth just swallowed the rest of him up?"

Nobody else smiled. Dorsey hadn't heard the scream.

Hatch noticed Lemieux glance at Bear. The two men made eye contact, and Bear gave the slightest hint of a nod. Hatch wasn't sure if he liked that look. He didn't like being left out of the conversation, whatever the hell it was that they were scheming. But he knew men like Dorsey, too, and liked his comment even less. The bureau people – creating policy disconnected from consequence, providing answers to questions no one asked, offering opinions without insight, and cracking jokes no one laughed at.

"Look guys, I was only kidding," Dorsey said.

"I think you're on to something," said Bear, but he offered no silly grin when he spoke.

A minute passed in silence. "Look, it's getting late," said Hatch. "Let's talk about it at the station."

"This is the time of day Parker went missing?" Bear asked.

Hatch gave a quizzical look, and nodded, "Yes, but ... "

"We'll be along, then," Bear interrupted him. "I need to think here, and Lemieux can show me the way."

Hatch hesitated, wanted to tell them to forget it and come with him and Dorsey. He wasn't feeling that good about leaving them there as it grew darker. As things turned out, he was right, but he had no way of knowing it at the time. He didn't believe in woodland-dwelling demon creatures, let alone in conjuring them up. They didn't exist. So, with reluctance, he said, "All right, but don't be too long. God knows we've had one too many search parties this summer."

"Wait," said Dorsey. "I think I'd like to stay and think with these two."

"You should probably go while you can," said Lemieux. He meant that in every meaningful sense of the words. "We could be a while."

"No," said Bear, "It would be good for him to stay."

Hatch shook his head. "Come on, this is nonsense. I need to report in at the station."

"You should go, Mr. Hatch," said Bear. "Report in. Let them know we made it this far."

Dorsey looked at Hatch and rolled his eyes. "I'm good," Dorsey nodded.

Hatch walked off disgusted. With each step he took toward the station he grew increasingly annoyed. After a couple of minutes, he turned. His intention was to go back and insist they accompany him to the station and they'd pick up the investigation tomorrow morning in the light. That was his intention, but he was quickly distracted by the sound of three loud knocks, like the sound of wood on wood. "Those foolish bastards," he thought. "Dorsey will have our jobs." He picked up the pace and took several steps back in their direction, but stopped short when he heard the faint echo of three more knocks filter through the forest. As he stood there, confused, he felt a sudden uneasiness about him. He took several more steps, but something inside told him to stop. A wave of dread and panic struck him. He wasn't alone, something was nearby. He could feel it. The forest felt it, too. For all at once, all around him was void and silent. Not a sound could be heard. The energy had been sucked out of the air and pulled in the direction of the three men back down the trail. He seemed hypnotized, and felt a pull in that direction, but resisted, and thanked God for the power to resist being pulled in. He was left to only wonder what could have possibly happened in those few minutes – that short span of time – when he walked away disgusted from Lemieux, Bear, and Dorsey, until that moment when he heard the unearthly, wicked savage scream of the damned, and how it shattered the silence of the forest.

This is what we know to be true – that and where they found the three mounds of salt on Misery Gore Trail. Oddly, in the exact same spot where they'd found Parker's hat and radio.

Hatch wrote down all he could at the station, waiting out the night for help to arrive. They found him there, on the floor, laid out cold. He had locked himself in. That was evident. The heavy wooden door was bolted shut and they had to gain access by shattering one of the small cabin windows. Whatever had attacked that door had left it a mess – gouged and mauled, cracked and splintered, with deep claw marks up and down and across the thick hardwood panels. Somehow the door had held, but not so Hatch's heart. Whatever truly happened – whatever he saw come at that door – we may never know – unless you believe those final words he wrote down – at the bottom of the paper in a shaking, trembling hand, "The thing is real – a Wendigo has risen – and it has found me."

* * *

After Scoutmaster Brown finished the tale, the silence lasted for several minutes. I remember hearing a few short gasps and a few more deep sighs from some of the scouts. I heard embers pop and crack in the fire. Crickets chirped. That I heard. And one of the owls, too, from across the pond, hooted, which only added to our somber, spooky mood. But no one spoke, which is what Mr. Brown intended, I think. He wanted

11

to let the story roll around in everyone's head. It had that affect on us. When he finally did speak up, it was to warn us all.

If only we all had listened.

"Never knock thrice upon a tree," Mr. Brown said, "In the dead of the forest on a summer's eve. For a knock in kind will come. When it does you should surely run as fast as you can. It's a call to the dead to rise and go forth, and take whatever creature it can possess back to the hell from where it came." Now the giggles finally came from the older boys. They came to an abrupt halt when Mr. Hall, the chaperon, who had stood in the shadows throughout Mr. Brown's entire tale, swung a thick limb we'd gathered for firewood and whacked it against the side of a tree. The knock was loud and echoed throughout the forest. He did it again, even harder, before Mr. Brown could raise his hand in a fleeting effort for him to stop, pleading in a whisper, "No – seriously – Roger!" But it was too late. He did it a third time.

That knock echoed, lingered in a vacuum and bounced through the forest for what seemed an eternity. Maybe it was the wind that carried it, the light breeze that danced through the tree tops that somehow pushed it on.

A vacuum, yes, that's what it would remind me of later. How the forest grew silent on that third knock. The maestro of the Great North Woods had waved his baton for the symphony of the night to cease, as though all sound had been sucked out of the air. Crickets stopped chirping. The owls stopped hooting. The distant, forlorn howl of a coyote fell silent. Bullfrogs at the pond croaked no more. The moths fluttering around the campfire vanished into the night. The buzz of mosquitoes stopped abruptly. When the silence was complete, when all had stilled, we heard the most dreaded sound I thought I had ever heard in my life. Three knocks in kind answered Mr. Hall's call, followed by a terrifying shrill cry.

"All right boys," Mr. Brown shouted out with a clap of his hand. "It's late – time for everyone to get in their tents and zip 'em up tight." At first, everyone was looking at each other confused. "Now!" Mr. Brown shouted. "Get in your tents!" We all got up and did what we were told – everyone but me. I was so nervous I went over behind a bush to relieve myself. I stood close enough to Mr. Brown and Mr. Hall to see and hear them, but just far enough in the shadows that they could not see me.

"Damn you, Roger," I heard Mr. Brown say to Mr. Hall. At first I thought it was a joke. It had to be, but then I saw the look on Mr. Hall's face, which looked like it had turned to wax. "We gotta salt the perimeter."

"I … I didn't know, Phil," replied Mr. Hall.

"We gotta do it as soon as these kids get in their God-danged tents like our lives depended on it," Mr. Brown's voice began to rise in a near panic. "Oh, by the way – it *does* depend on it Roger!"

"I … I thought you were bullshitting, Phil."

"Bullshitting my ass!" Mr. Brown snapped. "Gordon Hatch was my uncle, my mom's brother, and we still have that fucking notebook!"

"Why in God's name did you tell that story then, Phil?" Mr. Hall asked. "If you thought it was true or real or whatever?"

"I'm asking myself that same question now," he answered. "I just wanted to make a point to the boys about the importance of keeping an open mind because there is more out there than we know of, and use the fact that Hatch was my uncle to drive it home before you did what you did, Roger."

Mr. Hall had no response. Was he feeling like that man Dorsey did in the moments after Bear summoned the thing? About how this could not be real if he didn't believe in it? Could that have been what he was thinking … if any of this made sense … if any of this is to be believed?

I don't know why I did what I did next. An impulse, probably. There was a pine tree on the other side of the bushes – safer than a nylon tent, I reasoned. The low, thick branches hung in front of me like a ladder. As soon as I zipped up my pants I quietly climbed the tree. Grabbed and pulled and stepped upward until I came face-to-face with a fisher cat. The thing could have ripped my face to shreds. I came close to screaming out in fright. But the way it looked at me, its eyes in the soft glow of the firelight below, it was as though it recognized that it was in our mutual interests to remain quiet. Just like that, the fisher cat made room – snaked down to the outside end of the branch to let me sit at the trunk end like our lives depended on it. As it hunkered down into a ball of fur, I wondered how much it sensed or how much it knew of what was out there.

From where I was perched I could see most of the campsite, and as moments went by I could hear the tents zip up one by one. I watched Mr. Brown go to his tent and pull a small sack from it.

"Passamaquoddy Bay distilled and blessed – never thought I'd need it let alone test it," he said. Mr. Hall's eyes widened and bulged at Brown's words. "But I've brought it with me on every camping trip since the day they found Uncle Gordon."

Mr. Hall looked like he was about to go into shock, and it was only through Mr. Brown's urgency and prodding that he finally snapped out of it. The two went at it and worked fast. There was frantic energy about each man as they pushed themselves, sprinkled salt evenly on the outer edge of the campsite, and then around every tent. They made quick time of it – not that it was a day's work. There were only fifteen of us. Still, they seemed to finish just in the nick of time.

Mr. Brown's head jerked left before I heard the first sound. A snap of a branch, and then another. "Hurry up, Roger," he said. Mr. Hall was beneath me, sprinkling salt heavily on the ground, on the bush were I'd gone, and around the base of my tree. I should have listened to Mr. Brown. I wished I was hiding in my tent because when it came, it came with a force of nature – a wicked savage primordial scream that terrified me to my core. I was only fourteen, but in that moment everything I had ever believed to be fiction and the stuff of fantasy abandoned me.

"Dear God!" Mr. Hall breathed. "I hope you're right, Phil." He was panting nervously, staring into the dark forest.

"I hope I am, too," Brown replied wearily, resigned to his fate.

I could hear some of the other boys whimpering now – I was close to whimpering myself. If they hadn't believed this was real they did now. Not a one of them stuck their heads out of the tents. If they had, they would have seen what I saw.

The faintest, chalk-blue light appeared down the trail. I saw it move slowly, the light, not a form, coming our way. What Mr. Brown did next was nothing short of one of the most selfless acts of bravery I have ever witnessed. "Get in your tent, Roger," he said, "and zip it up tight."

"But Phil!" he pleaded.

"Go – now!" he said.

Mr. Hall did as he was told. When he had zipped up, Mr. Brown went up to the very edge of the perimeter they had formed around the campsite. That edge, facing down the trail, was directly below me. I could make out something in his hand, but I was unsure what. What I *was* sure of was that the thing had now moved directly down the path. The chalk-blue light was larger, brighter, and closing in on us. Mr. Brown stood defiantly below me. He stepped outside the perimeter now like he was drawing it in, letting it come toward him.

And it did.

It approached slowly, dragging one foot, its left one, which each step in our direction. The thing was ghastly pale, near naked, and hunched forward. Pants were torn and tattered. Boney, its skin so thin I swear I could see through it. Its arms hung lifeless to its knees. Blistered and open, festering sores covered its emaciated body – all across its chest and arms and face. Tufts of hair were scattered on its scalp. Its cheeks were hollowed out. Most disturbing of all was how its jaw hung unhinged, its tongue lolling over thin, dark blue lips. I gasped in fright. Mr. Brown slowly shifted his head up and spotted me, but returned his gaze to the thing immediately.

"Holy shit!" I heard him breathe. "Why-oh-why!" He dropped his right foot back and turned his torso slightly, stood in a boxer's pose, prepared to fight. "Don't move," he whispered to me, his eyes fixed on the specter before him. That fisher cat's claws could have swiped my ass and I wouldn't have made a peep let alone a move.

I could only imagine what was going through his head. Mr. Brown had been married to the same woman for over thirty years. He had three grown children and five grandchildren. He had been a scoutmaster through it all and he stuck with it even though his own kids were long grown and starting Cub Scout packs of their own by this time. He loved teaching us the way of the world – the way of the North Woods of Maine. He knew more about the forest than anyone I have ever known and surely he was the only white man who ever had carried a sack of Passamaquoddy blessed salt into the wilderness in the event that a moment like this one should come. He made a believer out of me that night.

I watched him lower his hand, waiting, anticipating, until that last possible second.

The thing arrived. Its lifeless arms moved and it lifted its bony hand and swiped at him, but Mr. Brown had expected that and stepped back within the circle. The thing hissed, but stepped no further.

"Come on, you spawn of Satan," Mr. Brown snarled.

It raised its hands slowly again. Its fingers were long and bony and the nails as good as talons. The thing lashed out quickly in his direction, just missing him. I was terrorized beyond comprehension. I still am. There was no way out then, and there is no way out now. I cannot escape the memory. In that moment it must have sensed my energy. With a sharp, mechanical twist of its neck it suddenly looked up at me and wagged its tongue playfully – diabolically – and pointed one of its hideous fingers at me.

Mr. Brown's hand moved back ever so slowly while it teased me. At first I thought he was going to punch it – coldcock it – as if that was possible. The thing sensed that, too, I think. It stepped back and began to move around the edge of the circle, trying to find a gap maybe, an opening to enter, but it kept coming back, swiping at Mr. Brown and hissing and tormenting me.

It went on that way for minutes, when suddenly, without warning, it struck in my direction like it had found a breach. Beneath me, it grabbed a lower branch of the tree, a branch that extended outside of the circle of salt. It shook the branch hard. The whole tree began to shake violently. The fisher cat's claws fully extended and dug deeply into the branch, but I lost my grip. Desperately I tried to grasp the trunk, but found nothing but air … and fell … straight at the creature.

The thing released the branch and lunged for me. Its jaw hanging unhinged and its mouth salivating.

That last possible second had finally arrived. Just as the thing had me within its grasp, Mr. Brown let fly a cupful of the salt – that's what he had hidden in his hand – and it landed squarely on the creature's face and upper torso. It fell back writhing in agony. I'm not certain if the scream that followed might have pierced the heavens, but I'm damn certain it pierced hell. That was the last thing I heard before I slammed into the forest floor.

The entire world was lost, then.

When I came to I convinced myself it was a bad dream. That was how I learned to live with the memory.

No one ever spoke of that night – ever.

I've struggled to find my way since.

And yet, here I am.

Around a campfire on a summer's eve I told my tale – Marlene smiled and laughed and picked up pieces of firewood, one in each hand.

She knocked the pieces together three times.

Loudly.

Even after I told her not to.

I regret I let her have her way. I will to the end of days.

We laughed as lovers do in less time than any lovers ever had when the forest answered in kind.

From the depth of a hellish place came the scream.

Where we sit our campsite is just a few paces off the trail – seven or eight strides, maybe. The air pressure has shifted. The forest has completely stilled. Embers in the fire pit glow bright amber beneath a blaze that weaves long spidery web-like shadows deep into the ink dark forest that envelopes us. Then and there I think it's a good time to run, even though we would be running into the pitch black night. On a trail covered in roots and rocks and God knows what else.

I say as much to her, urgently.

Marlene gasps ever so slightly then, and squeezes my hand tightly, painfully. She cannot speak, but tries to form the words in her mouth.

I look into her eyes, the fire light is flickering in them, but there is something else there, too, another reflection – a pale, bluish-white light. She is staring down the path, the way we had hiked in just hours before. I follow the direction of her eyes. What they are fixed on.

I realize how this story, if not my own, must find its own end.

By and by, come what may: woe be the one who finds this place where such a wicked savage tale, twice foretold, did pass upon a time in Maine.

People talk in hushed whispers of strange creatures that float out of the north woods and drift down east. One such tale settles uneasily into the hearts and souls of all who live, love, work and play upon the shores of the Lost Kingdom of Moose Harbor.

That Winged Thing

It's hard to believe that two years have passed since the town's strange encounter with that large winged creature. It was Halloween, late in the evening of October 31, when the reports started filtering in throughout town ...

Two couples in a minivan were coming from the moe.Republic Hotel's Halloween bash when they drove past the old Pratt Sawmill, its phantom shell illuminated in the pale moonlight. The driver, Sheila Quigley, glanced at the old works as she sped past, bewitched by its eerie, cold emptiness. Her lapse was momentary, broken by the sudden shouts of her companions. There in the middle of the road was a shadowy figure, standing on two legs, at least seven or eight feet high. At first they thought it was a prank. It had huge feathered wings folded across its back and two very large eyes, brilliant as emeralds, made more so by their illumination in the van's headlights. In its arms it held what appeared to be a good-sized dog. Sheila slammed the brakes, causing the van to do a three-sixty, and was about to plow into the creature when it rose up, actually flew away into the night. The passengers jumped out of the van and watched it fly away, but lost sight of it after a few seconds.

What they didn't know was that old Malcolm Glover had called the Downeast Way Police Department an hour earlier, around 9:30. Glover, a widower, lived up in an old farmhouse off Mountain Road, nestled in under Uriel's Ledge. He had been watching a hockey game on television when, as he said, he lost control of his set. The volume went haywire, he would later say. First, white sound filled the room, followed by a low, distinct voice. Barely audible, but oh so clear, "Leee-ave," it breathed in a deep, airy baritone. All at once, he found himself watching the hockey game again. At first he thought he had fallen asleep and was awakened by the old hoot owl that perched nightly on the high ledge. But he was awake and that was no owl. His dog, Nutcracker, a border collie mix who was on the front porch, began to bark when something thrashed loudly in the barnyard. Glover went outside without caution, thinking he, too, as the van load of revelers would assume an hour later, was a victim of an elaborate Halloween prank.

He saw Nutcracker, with her familiar red bandanna tied around her neck, facing the barn, which lay across the wide yard. She was now growling ferociously. The dark, thick hair along her spine stood on edge. It made Glover smile, thinking that the prank was about to turn on the prankster. He turned his flashlight on and scanned the barnyard. He moved the beam across the yard slowly and stopped when he spotted two large greenish eyes, luminescent and blinking, peering out from over a row of bushes near the barn door. Malcolm stands a good six feet high. The bushes, he realized, about a dozen mature sea roses, peaked above his eyes. Malcolm gawked at the phosphorous-like orbs that overwhelmed the featureless face behind them. They were set in a head that rested on broad shoulders, which were graced by, or what looked like … wings?

That was all the dog could take. Highly protective, Nutcracker bolted toward the barn. Glover called for the dog to stop, but it sprinted into the darkness. Turning into the house for his shotgun, the old man heard the dog screech loudly, painfully. That's when he called the police, then nervously went outside with his gun and flashlight. He scanned the yard with the light. The green eyes were gone and Nutcracker had disappeared. He lowered his flashlight and gazed above, up near the jagged ledge. In a fleeting instance he saw a flash, two green dots, like a pair of fireflies hovering over a meadow. And then a silhouette resting on the ledge … No, that couldn't be possible, he thought.

A few minutes after Malcolm Glover stood terrified on his porch, Margaret Connor and a few girlfriends had just left a screening of *The War of the Worlds* at Bud's Bijou Theater. There were dozens of people filtering in and out of the movie house when they spotted a "funny greenish light" that hovered high in the sky above Market Square. They stood watching as it turned down Brighton Lane towards the theater. "It wasn't an airplane," Margaret recalled. "No one could figure out what it was, but then, no one gave it much thought." It flew out of sight quickly, sinking behind the row of low buildings.

A couple of minutes later the women arrived at the lot behind the theater and piled in to an Oldsmobile. They started the car. The music blared out so loudly from the radio it startled them all. Then the radio tuner moved across the dial on its own, stations faded in and out evenly, before stopping at the end of the spectrum. White sound filled the car. Deafening at first, then spelled by an airy, deep vibration that seemed to pulsate through the car's speakers. At that instant, before their eyes, a tall, winged figure rose up in front of the automobile. "It was as though it had been crouching there hiding," Margaret would tell the police. "It came up slowly from the hood of the car. It was huge, wider and taller than a man, sinewy and muscular, with haunting, pale green eyes. It kept rising, too, right above the car. It held out a dog with a red bandanna, which lay limp under its left arm, like it was trying to give it to us." The women were scared and began to scream. Margaret, who was driving, quickly hit the door locks. When she put the big old GM in gear it stalled. They were trapped and, they were certain, facing their doom. The creature peered into the windows of the car looking at them closely, as though examining them under a microscope. The radio's strange pulsing vibration increased to a high pitch. Each woman could hear it plainly through the speakers.

There were at least a dozen people who were in the vicinity of the lot watching in stunned disbelief, amazement, and horror at the spectacle. The thing turned at them when the wail of police sirens alerted it. The creature rose quickly and ascended into the night, heading out toward the harbor, still clutching the dog. If this was a prank it was well staged. It defied the law of gravity and all known order of species in this and any ecosystem on the planet. By the time the authorities arrived the thing had vanished. Chief McO'Fayle heard the same story he had heard from Malcolm Glover, who was sitting in the front seat of the chief's Commando. Was he really supposed to believe a winged thing was on the loose?

By now the news of a strange winged creature was spreading all over town. Everywhere it seemed but the moe.Republic Hotel, which still was deep in revelry from its annual Halloween ball. The crowd was dressed in wild, outrageous, and frightful costumes, and was so big it had spilled out onto the side porch overlooking Moose Harbor. When the lights went out and the music stopped abruptly, at first the party-goers thought the interruption was part of the evening's festivities. The flicker of candles in a dozen or so jack-o-lanterns and the silvery moonlight cast ghostly shadows across the faces of the revelers and along the ground.

Then, above the murmuring and growing confusion there rose a low, but distinct, sound. A vibration pulsated in the air, coming from the lawn off the side porch. The throng, startled, reeled in horror simultaneously, when from nowhere, across the yard, a tall man-like figure with broad wings could be seen aloft. Its eyes flashed green in the dim light, "like reflectors on a mailbox," one witness would say, and it was gliding in right at them. The creature alighted softly at the end of the porch. There was something in its arms, limp and unmoving, what they soon recognized as a dog. The thing shuffled towards them slowly. People retreated in fear and apprehension. Just as it placed the object down, there came a booming thunderclap from up on the mountain,

22

akin to a sonic blast. It shook the grounds around them. The winged thing then lifted and glided away into the night. The power returned. Lights flooded the porch. That was the last sighting of the creature.

Whatever it was or may have been, it seems clear, by the number of witnesses, that it was very real. But was it something of this world? Everybody had their own explanation – a parasailing hooligan, a jet packed maniac, a large bird-like creature, even an alien visitor – but none more so than Malcolm Glover. He arrived at the moe.Republic Hotel with Chief McO'Fayle moments after the creature's departure. He had been with the Chief chasing the reported sightings all over town. They ran up to the porch where the guests, in stunned silence, had huddled around the dog, which lay still. Malcolm knew that it was Nutcracker. He recognized his border collie with the red bandanna immediately.

Just about everyone knows old Malcolm, and Nutcracker, too. That's why everyone was baffled and bewildered at what they saw, and then heard. Because at that moment the chief's two-way radio broke the silence. The dispatcher screamed loudly, excitedly, that Uriel's Ledge had collapsed above the farmhouse off Mountain Road right after that thunderclap. Malcolm Glover's house had just been obliterated under tons of granite. The ledge had simply cracked, a fissure, the state geologist would later report. She made no mention of what was left on that ledge. What did that have to do with the fact that the old house was flattened instantly? Other than the old man and his dog would have been crushed if … it hadn't been for that … winged thing.

Malcolm looked down at the dog, which all at once became alert and began to lick its master's face. People stood in wonder, some in doubt. Yet, incredible as it seems, it's all true. True as the color of Nutcracker's coat, which from that day forward was an oddly pale shade of gray. The queer thing was, come each full moon, the fur took on a starry, silvery hue that radiated in the night. People would say she'd been touched by moonbeams on that flight. Enchanted by that winged thing. Malcolm would only laugh. There were no further explanations necessary. Not about the creature, anyway. Or why it came. He knew what it was. Those who were there would agree. They'd seen it with their own eyes. The two of them, man and dog, had been saved on that Halloween night, not by a winged thing.

What then, you ask? Just look up on the ledge. It's there, your answer, high above, jutting out, to this very day. For all to see. Just as plain as the first time Malcolm had seen it. A silhouette which appeared before him in that instant. How else would you explain it? That when the wall of granite collapsed, all that remained above was that formation. Eerily precise. Clinging to the precipice. Forever watching over the Lost Kingdom. Its wings expanded. A fiery sword in its hand. Out of the rock a perfect sculpture of the archangel himself. Uriel, the guardian of the ledge.

*Each evening at an old resort in the Woods of Maine, a vacationer sees
an odd old man appear from the ether and hike up a trail that goes
nowhere – until one night when at last he's compelled to follow.*

Where Did He Go?

It had been gnawing at me for days, as frantic as a beaver making its way
through a grove of aspen. There was no end in sight, at least not for me,
as to when I'd wrap my head around what it was eating me. Restless
and uneasy, I couldn't let go of the sensation that something was
forgotten, missing, or lost. Not a way to spend the week at the Kineo
Mountain Lodge. I'd come here to relax and vacation. I'd waited a year
for this – fishing, boating, hiking in the Maine wilderness – and now I
was wired.

When I was a kid, whenever this happened, my mother always said,
"Martin! Never rush from the house to get where you're going or you'll
never get there without leaving something behind. Sit for a moment,
dear, clear your head – collect your thoughts – and you'll get where
you're going with a peace of mind – or at least a piece of your mind!"
she'd add with a laugh.

I'd wished I'd listen to her today, because even though I was sitting
peacefully on the back porch of the Lodge, sipping an ice cold beer,
reading a newspaper, and glancing at the lake front and watching the

sun set slowly over the mountains beyond – I could not relax.

I could only blame *him*.

For the better part of a week I had watched the old man hike up the trail behind the lodge. The trail crisscrossed skyward, more like a steep terrace, going up at a ferocious grade to the heights of a ridge line covered with cedar and hemlock. The first night of my stay, I noticed him appear from around the side of the lodge and hit the trailhead. I was on the back porch with my nose in a newspaper, glancing at the headlines, reading a paragraph or two as I went through it. The Sox had won, stocks were up, a moose-car collision had claimed two, a hiker had gone missing in central Maine, and the bungling Clouseau of a president had once again stuck his foot in his mouth.

I had just happened to pause from reading when the old man caught my eye. At the distance, I couldn't catch his face. Though he was bald on top, thick white hair rimmed his head, and he walked with a slight stoop as though he was searching for something ahead of him as he moved. It reminded me of a homeless man scouring for empty bottles in an alleyway, hoping to find a stash of empties to cash in at the redemption center. Both the white hair and the stoop hinted at his age. Maybe it was because of that, his age, or that he could still hike up that hill stooped as he was, or at the time of day he did it. Yes, all three – that's what got my attention. Here was this old guy, in the lingering twilight, near dusk, taking the hill in long strides. Gradually, between the light and dark, he melted into the forest.

The next evening, I was walking through the front lounge off the side of the lobby when I casually noticed him pass beneath a bay window that looked out on the lake. I should say I saw the darkly tanned crown of his bald head pass underneath a bay window. I was going in the direction of the back porch with a beer in one hand and the paper in the other, but by the time I reached the porch he was already well on the trail. He had my attention, but only later did he pique my curiosity.

In the Woods of Maine at summer solstice time, the sky to the northwest holds it light until close to ten o'clock. That night, I was on the porch until the sky had faded black and stars had punched through. Only then, as I walked inside for a nightcap, did it strike me. He had not returned. It's not like there was another trail off the ridge – not unless you bushwhacked it. The trail ended on a rocky promontory overlooking the lake and the mountains beyond. The drop was hundreds of feet. If he didn't hike back, where then, did he go?

If you're wondering why I didn't go up to him and introduce myself, so am I. Other than going to the trailhead and waiting there – and I did consider that – I never laid my eyes on him throughout the day. Truth was, at any given time of day it was easy to lose track of anyone amidst the crowd at the Kineo Mountain Lodge, an older gem built in another time and place. On a map, it was just north of central, up in the Woods of Maine. The lodge was a classic, rustic sprawling log cabin with grand rooms, a massive hall and wide wraparound covered porches front and back. The place was very popular in these parts. For starters, there was something for everyone – in addition to the fantastic hiking on and around the property that I partook in, there were tennis courts, badminton, croquet, and horseshoes. Evening meals were grilled on a barbecue. Though the big lake was well known for its boating and fishing, a nice little sandy beach on the property lured swimmers and sunbathers, too. The lodge also offered moose safaris, something I really enjoyed for the adventure of it all.

I had vacationed here for the past decade, every year during the last week of June. On vacation, I stayed active but enjoyed a few vices. I liked ice cold beer in the late afternoon to quench my thirst. In the early evenings, after dinner, I'd retreat to the back porch to enjoy a glass or two of Irish whiskey and a smoke. The whiskey was for my soul and the cigar kept the black flies and mosquitoes at bay. It was there, from my perch in an old Adirondack chair, that I'd first seen him cross the side lawn toward the trailhead and take off up the ridge.

On the third night, things got a little crazier. I was out back reading the paper and enjoying my vices, when I saw him hit the trail near dusk. As I watched him, a couple appeared in the wicker chairs to my right, holding hands as lovers do. Their eyes were focused on the old man, too, I noticed. They were speaking to each other. I could see their lips move, though I could not hear what they were saying. She pointed at the ridge and I was certain they were speaking of him. I was sure of it, and was about to say something to them to that effect – about how every evening at this time the old man just shows up and hikes the trail. Then he pointed at something excitedly, saying something to her. I followed his hand and stood up. "Holy shit, a moose," I said, maybe a little too loudly, and stepped forward. The old man was out of sight and a big bull moose was ambling up the trail. Amazed, I turned around to share the moment with the couple, but they had already left. I turned and looked back up but the moose had also slipped out of sight.

It happened so fast. I sat down slowly, taking it in. Nobody else seemed to notice the moose but that couple who showed no interest and simply disappeared. I leaned back in the Adirondack. I sipped whiskey and puffed on my cigar as mosquitoes buzzed my ear. I waited and watched patiently until ten-thirty. I'd like to say I'm not one to fret, but that night is when the gnawing sensation began to really take hold of me. As I read the paper, I learned that the lost hiker was still missing, but one of his sneakers had been found covered in blood. People were talking foul play now, which made me pause. That kind of stuff never happened up here in the woods.

Seeing the moose like that really got me thinking and I couldn't help begin to fear for the old geezer. I had heard a ranger speak once about safety in the Woods of Maine. One of the biggest problems in finding people gone missing in the woods is time itself. "It only takes a few days and that's it," he told us. It was a lecture, here at the Lodge, a few years back, and the talk had turned to a morbid fascination of people who disappear without a trace.

"In what way?" someone spoke up and asked him.

"Think of road kill, if you pardon the analogy, a deer, say. Hit by a car and left on the side of the road. The meat eaters work in shifts, from the large predators like bear, coywolves, and coyotes, down to the buzzards, skunks, weasels, flies and beetles. It takes about four days tops, and what's left may only be tufts of hide and a few bones."

I swallowed hard and thought of the missing hiker. Poor bastard. And then there was the old man. Was he at risk?

On the fourth night, he didn't disappoint, but came and went on schedule. After eleven, a vicious storm struck. For half an hour thunder and lightning exploded all over the grounds amidst a fantastic downpour. I could only wonder. After a nightcap, I went to bed and slept fitfully through the night. I remembered only fragments of dreams the next morning, and in my head I carried images of a faceless old man.

Sitting over morning coffee, reading the newspaper, I realized the mystery was fast becoming a mindless obsession. I was whiling away the hours of my vacation wondering about an old man I did not know, had no attachment to, and ultimately cared nothing about. For all I knew he could have been an eccentric forest-dwelling hermit or an astrophysicist who gazed at the Milky Way till dawn. This was the place to star gaze, after all, and that's probably what I should have been doing each evening rather than wondering about the old bastard. Why should I care about a senile old man?

That afternoon I decided to take a hike through the upper lake trail. I needed to clear the old man out of my head and getting in touch with nature was a sure way to do that. Forty-five minutes on the trail I came to a clearing that looked up at a barren, lonely mountain. As I stood there, I heard a sudden thrashing behind me and turned. An immense black bear was walking right up the path at me. I froze. There was nowhere to run or hide. It was that close. The animal sniffed in my direction. It looked to its left and right, took a cautious step toward me, approached with apprehension, and stopped short a few feet away. It sniffed again, and then looked into my eyes and began to growl menacingly. I was a dead man, I thought, so I did the first thing that came into my head. I spread my arms and growled back at the bear as loud as I possibly could. To my utter astonishment, the thing yelped like a startled puppy, turned and sprinted off into the forest.

At least I vaguely recall that happening. Because immediately after I growled I became lightheaded, woozy, my balance slipping. Suddenly, I felt as though I was falling, headfirst through a heavy mist. What passed for time seemed like hours until the ground rushed at me from nowhere and hit me hard. I opened my eyes with a start and had to breathe in deeply to catch my breath. My scalp was soaked in sweat colored blood red. A horrible nightmare, I thought, and sat up quickly, relieved to have escaped the void. But no – I found myself in a bone yard, naked and alone. In my arms I cradled a hollow skull. An empty bottle of Bushmill lay shattered on the ground beside me. I screamed in terror and woke with a jolt.

But I was alone and nowhere to be found.

That evening, the fifth night, I gave up waiting at my perch on the back porch. After I came to and wandered out of the forest dazed and confused, I went to the bar of the Kineo to gather my thoughts. That was too close a call. I was on vacation to relax and I really needed some stress relief. Few people were in the lounge, so I made a beeline to the bar and sat. But before I could even ask the bartender for a drink, a strange looking little man in a dark suit and fedora came up and sat on the barstool next to me. He was dressed like he had just arrived from a meeting at the *Daily Planet* or, the thought made me swallow, a wake.

"I'll have a beer and a shot of your finest whiskey," he said to the bartender. In a matter of seconds the order was placed in front of him. The strange looking little man thanked the bartender. Though I was slightly affronted, more at him than the bartender, I cleared my throat to order. But before I could speak, he slid the whiskey in front of me. "It's been a long journey," he said, and raised his pint. I stared at the whiskey for a second, then lifted it and met his glass with mine.

I took in the moment, not knowing what to make of it, the gesture, and him. His eyebrows were thick and bushy and gray as the hair around the sides of his head. All the more pronounced by his angular, bony cheeks and narrow chin. His nose protruded like the stunted beak of an old crow. It hung there precariously over thin lips pursed tightly. The fedora was tilted back on his wide forehead, the flesh of which was furrowed as long and deep as an Aroostook County potato field.

"Thank you," I said. "The name's Boudreau, Martin Boudreau." I waited an awkward moment expecting a reply in kind. Finally, I said,

"Here's to a long journey."

He took a deep pull on his beer, nearly half. Savoring it, he held the glass up in front of his eyes, and said, "The funny thing about journeys, even the longest ones must begin with the first step." He took another swig of beer. "That's the only way to get where you are going. On the other hand, as sure as that last step is taken, every journey must come to an end."

"You sound like a philosopher," I said.

"No," he replied, "But I was quoting one, or paraphrasing. I'm just a scribe, a reporter actually."

"No kidding? I was wondering." He really was dressed for the part – I had that right. As for him, the longer I looked the more he looked like a henchman out of a Grimm Fairy Tale.

"We follow a dress code. There's a certain amount of professionalism the job requires."

"That's interesting," I said. "What do you cover? The courts? The markets?"

"No, no," he answered. "I write about people." There was a hint of sarcasm in his voice, as he smiled slowly at the words, or maybe grimaced. I wasn't sure if he took pain or pleasure as he spoke. Even more so when he showed his teeth, stained the color of shellac. He shifted on his stool, then. When he did, the shadows across his face shifted, too. The changing light hit it from above and altered his features. His skin looked deathly pale all of a sudden, thin and cadaverous.

"Ah, that makes sense," I said. I couldn't take my eyes off his face. I thought I was speaking to a dead man. "Prob-probably why you're here," I mumbled and forced a thin smile when I said it.

"Yes, you might say that," he answered, and grinned that grin again. "When I'm on assignment, I like to meet the subjects I'm writing about – makes for a more interesting read."

"I … I can only imagine."

"Now, if you'll excuse me, I have to take a hike." He finished the rest of his beer in a gulp and stood. His face, now in a different light, had a little color. "It's time for me to get to work. There's a deadline to meet." He laid a twenty dollar bill down on the bar and left.

I watched him walk away, wondering what the heck that was about, but also feeling a little creeped out. There was something else, too, as he crossed the big hall. The realization when he turned the corner – the way he walked, his stoop. Seconds later I looked out the bay window and saw a black fedora bobbing under it. It was nearing dusk. I rushed to the back porch. At this point I needed to see if that was the old man or if this was all a bizarre dream in a macabre fantasy.

When I got there, the guy had already made the trailhead and was beginning his ascent.

So I did what any self-respecting obsessive compulsive busy body would do. I followed him.

I hit the trail for my own peace of mind. I wanted to see – had to see – where he was going or went to every night. I had to catch him. That's what I told myself. But within a minute, he was completely out of sight and I was sucking air and gasping for my breath. As a couple approached me I paused for a moment to let them pass and to catch my breath.

"Evening," the man said.

I gave a friendly nod and sucked wind, "More out of shape than I thought," I replied. "How much further?"

"You're almost there," the woman said. "A few more minutes at most."

"Thanks," I said. "Say, did you pass an old guy on your way down? He was just ahead of me a minute ago."

The couple looked at each other and shook their heads no. "Just now?" he asked.

I nodded. "Dressed like a preacher and looked like he stepped out of *The Scream*?"

They looked at each other again, but this time with concern. That look was familiar somehow, but I couldn't place it. "That's a painting," I added, " *The Scream*."

"We've passed no one," he answered.

"What he means is you're the only person we've seen coming down," she added. "But there was an older man up top." She pointed.

"He was there when we arrived, an hour ago," the man added, "An older guy in a dark baggy suit."

It couldn't have been him, I thought. "Odd looking fellow, a little creepy but friendly enough?" I asked.

She nodded. "With a black felt hat," she added.

"Really?" It simply couldn't be the same old guy.

"To tell you the truth, we were lost," the man said.

"More like confused," the woman added.

I couldn't disagree with that.

"About where to go," he said.

I looked up and down at the trail. In the twilight, it was very well groomed and clear of any debris. More importantly, there were still only two directions *to* go.

"But he helped us find our way," she smiled.

"He knows the area very well," the man added.

I had heard enough, and was just about to thank them, when the woman spoke suddenly, like she had fished out one last detail that would answer all my questions. In many ways, it did.

"He was a reporter, I think."

"How did you know?" I asked.

"He said he was glad we made it because he had a deadline to meet."

I stood there dumbfounded as they then walked past me without another word. I really didn't know how to respond or what to say. Should I say that it could be him? I turned to thank them but they were gone, had disappeared around a corner, I guessed.

Ten minutes later I neared the summit of the trail. I was rushing as fast as I could – too fast when I burst out on the promontory flailing to catch my balance. At the edge I felt someone grab me from behind, stopping me short of a swan dive. I took a sharp breath and turned but no one was there. No one. I did a three-sixty turn. No one. I began to look around again, but paused at the vista. The view, magnificent as it was, of the big lake dotted with dozens of islands, the sun slipping beneath the mountains, the endless forest, filled me with awe. I remembered how much I loved being here over the years. The beauty of the Eastern Frontier, a vast wilderness that still exists in a state of nature. But there are dangers, too, in nature, untamed and wild. The weight of it all struck me then. I let out a deep sigh and turned.

When he took off his hat I immediately recognized his bald crown. "Don't you have a deadline to meet?" I asked.

"Have you read the paper today, Martin?"

I nodded, "This morning, over coffee."

"Then you read the news."

I thought for a moment or two about what I *had* read – the Sox, the stock market, another presidential gaff, trade war looming, and … there was something else, too – a headline – but I couldn't see the words.

"It's been a long week," he said.

In my mind's eye, the headline began to focus, the block letters slowly forming.

"But they finally found you."

The words – they were almost there now.

"It was a trying week, what with the young couple and that moose, and then you. It took a while to get you all up here … to follow me."

My stomach began to pitch nervously, side-to-side like a ship rolling in a wild storm. My thoughts turned to the couple in the wicker chairs from a few nights back – realized it was them on the trail just minutes before – made the connection – and thought of the moose ambling up the steep trail.

"It's a big country, Martin. Your dreams will not be discarded. They are the fabric of the heavens. What they're made of."

Sweat welled up on my brow at the words. A single bead rolled down my temple. I could feel my heart beat rapidly. "Who … what are you?" I asked.

"A reporter. I told you."

"What the hell are you covering?" I shouted out. "Up here in the middle of the wilderness?"

"I cover people ... everywhere – tally up the sum of all the steps it's taken to arrive at their destination – and write their story."

I shook my head in disbelief. "What exactly is it you write, old man?"

He took a step toward me and placed a hand on my shoulder. "I write obituaries, Martin. I reap the journey of life and put it into words for all to see." In that instant, I looked into his eyes and saw the moment of my demise. "I am not old, Martin. I am ancient." He grinned that grin again. "I am the *reaper*."

The headline rushed up at me then – the big block letters came sharply into focus and I read them slowly: "Remains of Hiker Found, Victim of Bear Attack!"

Images pass in fractal. Thoughts come at me in unison. All the memories coalesce at once. I see the journey of my life for what it is. The good, the bad, the awkward and the awful, the best and brightest, the stupid and shameful, the wrong and right and regretful, it's all there. I am at *peace* with it all – the word turned in my head and made me smile – *peace*.

It's then I hear my mother's voice speak to me. Calmly giving me the advice she gave all those years before about collecting my thoughts before I leave to go anywhere. I realize mom had it right, at least about one thing – that "piece of your mind" she talked about. That's about all that was left.

*On a cold winter's night, a desperate and scheming man finds
his true self amid dark terrors inside an enchanted forest.*

Howlin' Minnie
The Witch of the Wailing Wood

I

Confusion overwhelmed him like a wary traveler, lost and alone, standing at a crossroad. He was face-down in a snowdrift and came up with a bloody lip and a welt across his face. Cursing, he wondered how many times he'd fallen. He'd lost track. The night had been a long one, and it took all his strength to pick himself up. Moon rays broke through the clouds and over his shoulder, reflecting off the fresh snowfall, dotting pale, bluish sparkles on the broad, rolling field where he stood. The luster offered bare definition to the dark forest that bordered the field. He took a step in that direction and paused. A coyote sang out suddenly, eerily, from up on the mountain, sending a shiver of fright through him. A foreboding gripped him, but he quickly shook it off. He took a deep breath and continued. Dawn had to be approaching, he reckoned. Maybe an hour, more or less, till the safety of daylight, but he was unsure. Time eluded him.

The traveler made out animal tracks in the snow. A predator and its prey had raced across the field not too long ago. The predator's tracks were large and deep. A coyote, most likely, despite the size of the print. The one which had just sung out was not that close. He wondered which animal had won, and then saw a stain of blood in the snow. That made him nervous. He didn't like being out here in the wild this late, alone, with hungry predators on the prowl.

"Moss Hunter, put the thought out of your mind," he said aloud, but he was not encouraged as he approached the trees on the edge of the field, standing tall like sentries. He knew he had no choice but to go there, to confront the forest and enter. It was the fastest way back to town, and he had to get there as fast as he could for Pritchard's sake. When he had left him after the accident, all warm and cozy next to a campfire, Moss figured that Pritchard had about two or three hours at the most before the fire died out. Then it would be only a short time in this weather before the frigid blast following the storm set in and Pritchard would become a block of ice. The last thing Pritchard had cried out was, "You'll never escape the Wailing Wood." Moss had laughed it off and replied, "I ain't afraid of Howlin' Minnie, Pritchard, if that's what you're thinking. Christ, I'm not a kid. Besides, a man in your condition, that's the last thing you should be worrying about, my friend."

Moss had continued to laugh as he'd trudged off. Anyone daring to enter the Wailing Wood after nightfall was risking life and limb, or so held the old superstition. That was her lair. Where she lay in waiting to claim the next soul as her own. Enter those woods after dark, it was said, and you would not see the dawn. No one had ever lived to tell about it in all the years since she had first appeared – 1845, on the one-year anniversary of the day they had found her after her "leap" from Parson's Drop. That's when Howlin' Minnie returned to claim these woods – with the power to unleash the divine and diabolical of the forest itself.

Every child in the Lost Kingdom of Moose Harbor knew the fate of Howlin' Minnie and how she came to be. The story was a near indoctrination, a ritual, for the young and old at every campfire, picnic, and sleepover. As the story went, her father, the Parson Amos Verde, had led his followers to the heights of the northern cliffs of Mount Agamenticus on the first day of spring in 1844. Parson Verde and his flock were Millerites, a religous sect that sprang from the Baptist faith after the Reverend William Miller prophesied the second coming of Christ. Claiming to use the power of science, reason, and deduction, he interpreted scripture to predict the Rapture would occur on March 21, 1844. Parson Verde came to believe the word of the Reverend William was divine and absolute. He had heard the Reverend William preach from the back of a hall down in Falmouth the year before. Parson Verde was so moved by the sermon that he felt he had been personally anointed by Reverend William to carry out the prophecy. In those times, much like most times, people tended to believe anything that was delivered with an air of veracity, authority, and reason behind it.

Parson Verde's plan was simple enough for his followers. The date and time of the Rapture had already been set. On the day of the Second Coming, his flock would climb to the heights of the northern cliffs that would later come to bear his name, and, at the precise moment, fling themselves off into the waiting arms of their savior. Parson Verde was so convinced that Christ would be waiting below to catch one and all in His bosom and carry them up to heaven, the parson was willing to sacrifice his lone daughter, Minerva, to be the first to leap into His waiting arms.

Minerva presented a problem for Parson Verde – a problem that stood between him and his spending all eternity in heaven. She, he was convinced, had placed his deliverance and eternal salvation at jeopardy. She was a sinner – a fornicator – wild and unruly, who had broken her vows of matrimony. She had been caught in the back of the church personally receiving and accepting the spirit of the Lord from an itinerant preacher, who was visiting the Lost Kingdom to preach by her own father's invitation. The affair was quite scandalous. Minerva's husband, Bunker Rangeley, was shocked and devastated, and their children were quickly ostracized by the community.

The affair so vexed Parson Verde that he came up with a plan to save poor Minerva's soul from eternal damnation. He convinced

Bunker that he could save his wife from the fiery pits of hell. With reluctance, and without receiving a full disclosure of the method of "baptism," Bunker agreed. Amos was overjoyed. He would save his daughter and himself for eternity, as he had from her early years on, when he regularly introduced the spirit of the Lord into her.

On the day of prophecy, at the appointed hour, she was cast into His arms from the heights of Mount Agamenticus. The people of the Lost Kingdom and beyond can testify that Parson Verde's flock was greatly disappointed when it discovered that its savior missed the Rapture that day – and poor Minerva. He was not there to catch them. It took two days to find the body. Deep in the forest, Minerva Verde Rangeley came to rest in the arms of an old maple tree, broken and twisted. A year later, on the anniversary of that find, Parson Verde went into the forest. The townsfolk believed it was to pray for his daughter. Or so it was said, for he was never seen again. From that day on, however, whenever anyone neared that stretch of forest after dark, the distant wail of the fallen was heard. The Witch of the Wailing Wood called, they said, to lure another sinner into damnation.

Moss was not taken to superstition, but there was always a but, a consideration, when it came to the Wailing Wood after dark. When Moss was a boy, a man named Dick Hartfield – who hunted these woods each autumn – was caught in an early nor'easter. Hartfield was not well liked. He had a temper and reputation as a drunkard and wife beater. Maybe that's why there wasn't much effort to look for him when he was reported missing. Nevertheless, they didn't find him – or what was left of him – until the following spring. "He didn't dress for the weather," Moss's mother and father had said. "You got to learn how to dress in these parts."

"When you go out in the cold, you need to dress right. You can always be too warm, but you can't be warm enough," his folks would tell him. "And you never know when a storm's going to blow, especially in the fall and spring." The one thing his folks never bothered to explain to him was why, when they found old Hartfield, he was dressed in enough layers to lead an arctic expedition. And that he was sitting upright against a tree with his legs crossed, his head forward, his jaw gaping like he had been frightened by something. People figured he tried to make it home – took a shortcut through the Wailing Wood – or got lost – and wandered too close to the tree. Her tree. She came for him and caught him. Claimed his soul and took him to hell. How did

they know it was her? A man's eyes are the windows to his soul, ain't they? That's what they say. Everyone knows no man can look into Howlin' Minnie's eyes without losing his. And that was the queer thing about the way they found old Hartfield, just as she had left him propped up against the tree – with hollowed eye sockets staring blankly into the abyss. There were others, too, that people spoke of, who over the years had strayed into the Wailing Wood and were found just like Hartfield – or were never found at all.

A cold wind rose up around Moss. It sent shivers through him. It drifted the powdered snow into finely whipped layers. Despite what he'd told Pritchard, Moss had weighed the prospect of seeing the dawn versus entering the Wailing Wood. Struggling now through a drift, twisting and pulling in the waist-deep snow, he cursed, thinking maybe this wasn't a good idea after all. Pushing forcefully, he finally broke free of the drift and onto a snowmobile trail that skirted the forest – the very trail he'd been on earlier that day with Pritchard. With that last effort, he made up his mind.

II

Laid out at the base of the northern slope of Mount Agamenticus, what came to be known as the Wailing Wood consisted of a heavily forested tract of hardwoods and white pine, cedar, and spruce. The wood marked the natural boundary between the Lost Kingdom of Moose Harbor and the wilderness beyond, which only added to its mystique and aura over the years. After an eternity traipsing and plodding through the wild to get there, Moss now stood at the forest's edge, contemplating one last time which path to take. He stared at the forest, knowing that he was only an hour's walk away from town if he followed the winding trail through the woods. If he walked the distance around the side of the mountain it would be another two hours before he made it to Mountain Road, then another half hour to the spot where he would come out if he followed the path through the wood he was standing on now. A pair of great horned owls hooted rhythmically from somewhere nearby. A coyote bayed deep within the forest. Another answered from the direction of the mountain. There was a momentary pause when a third animal responded with a chilling, shrieking call from the forest. Moss recalled reading something somewhere that coyotes signal each other with a shriek when a feeding opportunity arises. He remembered the large tracks he'd seen in the snow earlier, then the bloodstains, and shuddered.

That got him thinking. The path before him was visible. The forest parted invitingly. Pritchard was laid up a few miles back. After the accident, he had left him there, busted up but beside a pretty good fire. There was enough wood burning to hold him over until after daylight. He had to get into town and contact the chief, have him get a party back to Pritchard before the fire died out. He would then have to contact Louise, Pritchard's wife, and explain to her how Moss and Pritchard crashed the Ski-Doo into a tree. "Oh, he's okay," he would tell her matter-of-fact like and wink. "He's lucky. Actually, we're both pretty damn lucky we jumped at the last second while airborne." Then she would cry and scream obscenities like she was supposed to. She was a woman and that's what women do. Then Moss would have to endure the whole thing all over again with his missus, if she wasn't already there beside Louise when he told it the first time. "The throttle stuck," he'd explain. "Son-of-a-bitch throttle – and he couldn't brake it – came out of the turn too damn fast. I knew something was wrong, so I rolled off the back just before liftoff. He tried to hold it to the last second but jumped off airborne on the curve. The snowmobile went one way, he went another, and his ankle went another. There was no way Pritchard could walk out of those woods." That was the story they'd gone over. Moss wouldn't mention the fifth of Crown Royal – or that he, Moss, was driving. When you smash a $4,000 machine it's best to embellish the loss with a $10,000 story rather than a $20 bottle of whiskey. The owls hooted again, followed by a lonesome, high-pitched howl that carried on the wind. Moss hesitated longer. He took a deep breath. He thought about which way to go one more time. "This is ridiculous," he mumbled aloud, finally. "I'm a grown man," he said with conviction, and entered the forest.

For some reason he thought of that poem by Frost, the one about the path not taken – or was it the road not taken? Yes – two roads diverged in the wood, and the guy took the one less traveled by, which made all the difference. Something like that. He reached into his head to pull out the poem, but he could not remember it. Still, the diversion gave Moss some comfort as he walked down the path; he took longer and longer strides, confident that he would break through to the other side in no time.

He became distracted from his thoughts when he noticed that the path was changing, how it glistened more brightly the further he went into the wood. It grew in radiance, in luster – as though the moon was directly above and its rays were igniting thousands of silver sparks on the snow – lighting his way, guiding him. The second thing he noticed was the calm. A sense of relief passed through him, that he had made the right decision to enter the wood rather than walk another five miles around it. The third thing was the absolute quietude. He had been walking along, relieved for several minutes, thinking about the poem, when he realized that he'd left all sound behind upon entering the wood. No owl hooting. No coyote howling. No shrieks. And oddly, no wind. It was as though he had walked into a vacuum. He could hear the squeaky sound of his footsteps on the hardened trail, but that was it. A sensation struck him. A sensation that he was not alone. Was he being watched? Or, heaven forbid, followed? "Anyone there?" he shouted impulsively, regretting the slight the moment he spoke. Two knocks responded from somewhere in the forest. A single knock rapped loudly ahead of him, then three more behind him. The spirits of the wood, he had once heard, come knocking in the darkest hours. They were now communicating. Panic hit him immediately.

Pritchard would not be found if he didn't make it, Moss thought. It didn't matter how he made it into town! Moss turned to run – to sprint out of the Wailing Wood as fast as he could – to break the enchantment before it was too late. Convinced that everything about the place was real, his thoughts drifted to wild, man-eating carnivores, ghostly apparitions, and a ghastly, scheming witch. Maybe it's the fate of humanity that people cannot or will not listen to their hearts. All before them speaks, but they do not listen. Moss had hesitated before entering the forest but did not listen. Why in God's name had he not followed his heart instead of his head? There was no way back. No way out but the path before him. For when he turned, there was nothing but wood; the forest had consumed the path behind him, devouring the trail eagerly, hungrily at his heels. If he stood much longer, he reasoned, the forest would eat him alive.

There was no choice but to press on, even after three more knocks sounded behind him and two responded ahead of him. Nervous and unsure, he quickened his pace, thinking the best strategy was to distance himself from the thing behind him but not move so quickly that he'd run blindly into whatever was in front of him – for surely something was there . . . waiting.

A sound made him stop abruptly and listen. His heart beat rapidly in expectation. Was that the crunch of snow ahead? Someone or something was coming toward him. A terrifying thought suddenly entered his head. What if the forest was devouring the path from the other end? And that the speed with which it consumed the path was driven by the speed with which he ran? Unsure of what to do, Moss looked around and then up at the canopy of branches above him. The squeaky crunch of snow was now distinct and indicated movement coming directly toward him. He climbed into the canopy.

III

The figure appeared from out of the darkness, walking slowly, cautiously on the path as if it was searching for something on the ground. The radiance from the path cast the shadowy figure in a silvery hue as it moved closer to Moss. He noticed a rifle, the long barrel hanging inches from the ground. The figure was tracking, not searching. Coming up to the exact spot where Moss had stood, the figure stopped, crouched down, examining the surface area all around, and then stood up again.

"You best come down while you can," the figure called out. He then looked straight up into the branches above. Moss was laid out on one limb, balancing precariously, staring into the face of an older man. He could see days-old specs of gray stubble on his chin and cheeks. Deep wrinkles were stamped like crow's feet at the corners of his eyes. The old man was dressed in a plaid green wool jacket and matching cap with buckskin gloves. It reminded Moss of something his grandfather or great-grandfather had worn hunting. That was ages ago, he thought, entire lifetimes.

"Why should I?" Moss finally said. "How do I know you're not going to shoot me?".

The old man rolled his eyes and shook his head in disbelief. "Don't you think I could have done that already?" he answered. "Damn, son! You're treed like a raccoon and laying on that limb like a trussed hog on a spit. Now get down from up there before it's too late – those are treewolves on the hunt, and they're on the move." The old man stepped back and Moss lowered himself from the branch, dropping to the ground with a grunt.

"Who are you?" asked Moss.

"The wolves," he answered, ignoring him, "they're running in packs and on the prowl. They're big ones. Their shoulders are this high on me, son," he added, raising his hand above his waist, "and they're damn hungry, too. I caught sight of a small patch of bloodstains out in the field. Probably a rabbit, which means they're not having much luck. One scrawny rabbit isn't going to feed the pack. There are four or five of them running tonight, for sure."

That perplexed Moss and made him uneasy. The field was in the opposite direction from which the old buck had appeared.

"I didn't think wolves were in these parts," Moss said, eyeing him closely, noticing the pale glow of his skin. Further, what he didn't say – and that was mostly out of respect for the long-barreled muzzle the old geezer carried – was that a wolf, let alone wolves, had not been spotted in these parts for well over a hundred years. "You sure it wasn't coyotes you spotted?"

The old man looked at Moss for a moment suspiciously and then burst out laughing. "You almost had me," he said.

This confused Moss even more. "You mentioned something about treewolves?"

The old man stopped laughing abruptly. "These are no ordinary wolves, son. If they didn't look like a wolf I'd swear by the size and look of their print that I was trackin' black bears. They got claws is what I mean. They can stand upright. I've never seen anything like it, but that's how they climb trees, and how we've come to call 'em 'treewolves.'"

"We?" Moss asked. But before the old man could answer, a loud shriek – like what Moss had heard earlier – erupted from the woods.

"Follow me before they get your scent," he said with a nod to his right. The shriek exploded again and was followed by a long, doleful howl. "Dang – too late. Looks like they got your scent. They're locating each other and then they'll triangulate. It's how they hunt."

Fear welled up in Moss. But as he tried to calm himself, reason spoke to him. Don't be a fool, he thought. The shriek of a coyote is bloodcurdling. That's how the animals communicate with each other – probably just another rabbit. Yet what he had just heard was disturbing. And the large tracks that he'd seen in the snow earlier were very real. Where in God's name was the old geezer going to take him? How could he take him anywhere but back in the directon he came? But the old man didn't hesitate. He just walked by Moss quickly like he had somewhere to go. Right onto the path that had disappeared a moment before, that had been swallowed up by the wood at Moss's heels. Now it was clear, and the old bastard was making time. "Hurry!" he shouted, without a look back.

Another shriek and several howls erupted. Moss was near the breaking point. Whether from excitement or his own confusion – he really wasn't sure anymore – he followed the old man. Before long, Moss realized there was nothing familiar about where he was or where he was going. This was not the path he had just covered. There were no footprints on the fresh snow. The old man was leading him deeper into the forest, away from town and the field where he'd entered. Shrieks and howls again erupted – but louder.

"They're closing in," the old man laughed, "but they're not gonna catch us now." He stopped and pointed toward a narrow opening ahead of them and laughed again. Moss caught up, out of breath. There was a light breaking through the trees that he recognized as a campfire. "They're afraid of fire," the old man said.

"Good enough for me," Moss answered and began to move.

Before he took a step the old man grabbed his arm and said, "Not so fast."

What Moss saw next he could never have imagined. No one would have believed him. A wolf – or a creature that resembled a wolf, for its torso and tail looked like a wolf's, but its snout and jaws were elongated and exaggerated. Its paws were enormous, leaving little doubt that the thing could climb trees, Moss reckoned. When it made eye contact with the two men, the creature stood up erect on its hind legs, taller than both of them. The thing snarled ferociously. Its long claws were exposed – claws that could cut a person into five finely minced pieces with a single swipe.

"Let's go, sonny," the old man shouted, and he charged straight at the beast. Out of fear, insanity, or the fact that the old geezer had his rifle locked and loaded – whatever drove him – Moss didn't hesitate. Good thing. Out of the trees above where they had stood, two more "treewolves," or whatever they were, jumped down, just missing him. "Now it's an even fight," the old man yelled with excitement, running straight toward the creature that blocked their way. Moss was right on the old man's feet as the two beasts behind him were closing in on his. The geezer raised the barrel and fired on the run. The bullet struck the wolf-beast on its side, spinning it around and slamming it into a tree with a horrific yip. That was enough – enough space to get by and bust through to the clearing.

"Down," a voice shouted. Moss dove forward as the jaws of one of the beasts snapped savagely in his ear, frothing and spitting saliva in anticipation of the kill. A rifle fired above his head, followed by a painful, horrific yip and growl. He looked back and saw a pair of wounded wolf-things staggering backward defiantly, away from the light, into the darkness. A third stood tall for a moment and then dropped on all fours and leaped away. All around him, throughout the forest, shrieks and howls of the beasts that had nearly killed him rose. Were they retreating or encircling them?

"You okay there, brother?" asked a gaunt looking man. He was as pale as the old man, Moss noticed, though younger. He, too, wore a battered, frayed hunting jacket with matching cap, but it was red and faded. "You look like you've seen a ghost."

"That's not what I'd call that... those things," Moss said, his heart beating, fluttering, as he gasped for air. "I don't know what I'd call 'em. I've never seen anything like that."

"Treewolves?" the gaunt man said. "They're all over these woods, but they live secret-like. Nocturnal they are – can't stand the light of day. They've been known to creep into local farms occasionally for livestock, but that's only when they're desperate. Their only weakness is when they get the scent of fresh blood. Human blood. They're man-eaters." He grinned broadly, showing a row of pearly white teeth. "Your blood must be percolating real good because I ain't never seen them get this close to the tree of fire. It's about the only thing that'll kill 'em – send 'em back to the hell from where they came – if they enter the ring."

Moss looked around to get his bearings. The clearing was circular, a good twenty-five feet across. An old maple stood tall and leafless in the center. He had heard about old-growth maples growing ninety to a hundred feet high. This one easily topped that, and its girth was a good five feet, which meant the tree itself had to be hundreds of years old. "This tree's a landmark," he said aloud, just as the realization hit him. It marked the spot. The one where the preacher's daughter had landed when she was thrown from Parson's Drop. There was a small campfire blazing near the base of the tree and five torches ablaze, all evenly spaced around the perimeter of the clearing. Three more hunters stepped out from the back side of the tree, out of its shadow, as though from the tree itself. Each man looked the same as the other – pale, dully glowing skin that glimmered in the moonlight, with gaunt features, eyes dark and sunken, and a week-old growth of stubble on their faces. Like the other two men he'd encountered, the three wore shabby, old-fashioned plaid caps and coats, the colors faded. The circle in which they all stood was marked by a pentagram with the tree in the center and the torch lights at each point of the star. The ancient warding of evil or the invitation for evil? The symbol was not lost on Moss. "Where the hell am I?" he thought.

"Don't be frightened," the guy with the pearly whites said, as if he knew what Moss was thinking. "That," he pointed to the pentagram, "is what keeps the sons of bitches away ... works like a charm," he added as an afterthought. Then he flashed the big whites again.

Moss wasn't sure if he was trapped or saved. "Not be frightened?" he said. "I'm beyond frightened."

"Well, you can stay in here or go out there," the old geezer who'd found him said. "I can tell you this – no stray I've known of has made it out of these woods alive."

"I'm not a stray, old man," Moss replied sharply. "I know where I am and where I'm going. Do you?" It seemed as though the old man was about to reply sharply himself, but as he began to speak, to verbalize a response, he quieted. A dumbstruck gaze fell over his face. "I gotta friend laid up on the other side of the mountain," Moss pleaded. "He's gonna turn into a block of ice if I don't get back to town real soon and notify the chief."

The five men stared at him blankly, and then looked at each other. Finally, one of the other men spoke up, "You don't get it, brother. You can't leave now."

"No one ever leaves," another said.

"It's too late," Pearly Whites added.

"It's gonna be too late for Pritchard," Moss replied, thinking about the story they'd concocted. "If I don't leave."

"It's already too late," the fifth man smiled. His right eye was opaque, listless and dead. "You should know that." His gaze was oddly cold.

"I don't know what you're talking about," said Moss, confused, but the men's attention shifted. They fell silent, ignoring him. Their heads cocked slightly as though listening or struggling to hear something. A sharp wind responded. It streamed through the forest, dipping in and out of the crowns of trees. Echoes followed on the wind. A cry erupted – a woman – pleading, begging for mercy. Moss walked to the edge of the circle and scanned the wood, thinking the beasts were on the prowl and had cornered her.

"We've got to do something before they get her," Moss shouted excitedly, "before it's too late."

50

"It's already too late, brother," Dead-Eye said. "You know that. I just told you that." The men broke out in laughter. Pointing at Moss, mocking him. A woman's voice again carried on the wind – distant, then close. The men ceased laughing. Solemnly, they stepped toward the tree and turned. They each pressed their backs against the trunk, slid down uncomfortably, and sat cross-legged. They bowed their heads together and began to repeat the Lord's Prayer in unison. "Our Father, who art in heaven…"

Moss was beside himself. The wind kicked up, rising. More voices carried high through the treetops. "Hallelujah!" rang out in succession. A woman screamed for mercy. Moss shuffled wildly around the circle. A sense of urgency gripped him. "…lead us not into temptation; but deliver us from evil…" the men continued undisturbed. He went to the edge looking for a way out, peered deeply into the forest and was met by the gaze of red eyes staring intently back at him from all around. He took one step from the circle. Immediately, a beast sprang up in his face, growling savagely and swiping at him wildly. "Jesus Christ!" he shouted, falling back on his ass.

Moss caught sight of the old man shaking as he worded the final passage. "…For thine is the Kingdom…" Moss ran toward him. "What's happening, old man?" he yelled. "You know, don't you?" He grabbed for his head and yanked his hat off. Moss clutched the hat tightly. Holding it up, staring at the inside, he gasped. On the band, printed in large block letters old and near faded, the once dark ink read Dick Hartfield. "…the power, and the glory…" Moss swallowed hard, reached for the old man. "…for ever and ever. Amen!" and froze with his hand upon the man's head. The scream came from the heavens and swept through the forest. Moss could feel the wrenching pain, then ferocious rage build as the wail lingered. Seconds later, the old maple tree trembled and shook in spasms, as though it struggled for its last breath before giving up the ghost.

Moss freaked. "I asked you what's happening, old-timer! Tell me!" he yelled, grabbing the old man's gray, greased scalp and jerking it back. Moss reeled away in shock. The old man, what was left of him, was a lifeless corpse. The hollow, sunken, eyeless sockets were staring into the nothingness of time. His jaw hung, unhinged. An army of dung beetles flowed out his mouth, down his chin and neck. Moss nearly convulsed at the sight. He didn't have to look further to know the fate of the others. All the men were gone. That pearly toothed, poor bastard was right. It was too late ... for them. Frozen in time. Trapped in the circle of fire by what? The beasts or her? Were they one and the same? Throughout the wood, the wail drifted eerily from tree to tree, weaving near then far, growing in pitch. She was getting closer, coming for him.

Is it fear or desperation that finally triggers the human urge to survive? How many times must the spirit look into the abyss? How far must it fall? To be crushed by the weight of time? To be frozen in time? She was coming for him. The wailing was closing in. Moss collapsed to his knees, bent over, shutting his eyes tightly and covering his ears with his hands. He saw himself stand and dart past the beasts nearest him. Running wildly down the path he had followed with the old man. The snapping of branches and beasts at his heels. Where the beasts failed the forest would not. He dared not look back for fear of what lay behind. If he faltered, the forest, if not the beasts, would consume him. He would remain here. Frozen in time with the rest of them.

He saw all of this in an instant. Raising his head and dropping his hands to face his maker, Moss opened his eyes. There, on his knees, he found himself back on the hardened trail, looking at the winding path that led down the mountain into the Lost Kingdom of Moose Harbor. The forest had gone still. He knelt in silence as though in prayer. As before, a radiance and luster marked the path ahead. He glanced back with apprehension, and to his relief, he saw the path as it was – or was meant to be. He saw the packed trail covered in an unblemished dusting of light snow that had penetrated the canopy above.

He breathed deeply and stood up, pondering what had happened or what he'd imagined, whether he'd lost valuable time or not. How much time, if any, he had no recollection. But if he had blacked out, or had some kind of sensory breakdown, some hallucination brought about by the exposure to the elements, would there be time to make it to town and get back to Pritchard? What if it wasn't a hallucination, he thought? That made him shudder. If he continued on this path, this illuminated trail – its silvery sparks igniting invitingly – what awaited him around each bend? If he ran into one of those wolf-beasts, his end would be savage and gruesome. He decided to go forward, reasoning, what choice did he really have? He had made his choice. There was no turning back at this point. His life was set. Why should it be any different in death if it was meant to be?

Cautiously, he went down the brilliant path. The still of the forest frightened him. He picked up his pace, wanting eagerly to clear the wood. As before, he felt a presence begin to grow around him. He looked from side to side, expecting to locate red eyes gleaming at him in the darkness. Nothing was there but the night. He couldn't shake an overwhelming sensation of dread. The presence was on him, smothering him. The forest? The thought unnerved him. He swallowed hard. The forest, all around, was following him, watching his every move. A branch snapped. He turned sharply only to find the forest had closed in on him once again. "Who's there?" he shouted out. Immediately, a knock sounded from in front of him. Two more rapped behind and to his right. Three came from his left. Five knocks echoed in the far distance, from the direction of the tree. Moss stood wide-eyed. He wondered if the forest had already swallowed him alive. Had he entered an endless purgatory between heaven and hell? He was as doomed as Pritchard. Moss's sanity was slipping away. Ebbing out of him like a tide on a forgotten, far away seashore. What did this night hold for him?

From the darkness, the answer came. A long, lone, threatening howl. Seconds later, another howl responded from the opposite direction, then another from the other side, until a chorus erupted throughout the forest all around him. Envisioning the unthinkable, he remembered what the old geezer had said about the treewolves – the hideous mutant wolves – and how they locate their prey. There was no way for him to know if they were beside him or a mile away. He wanted to run, should have run, but found himself struggling to move. The effort was immense, as though he was plodding through the snowdrifts again. The menacing yowls intensified. Trapped in a nightmare, frightened beyond his wits, monsters closing in, he sought desperately to awake. To be gone from these woods.

The howling ended abruptly. Scared and nervous, Moss figured he was nothing more than dog food and that the mutant wolves had encircled him – were going to pounce on him and tear him to shreds. Strangely, he wondered if his life would pass before him. Does that really happen, he thought? If so, at what point does the projector roll? When he was being eaten alive and disemboweled? As his bones were being crunched? His limbs torn from him? Before he lost consciousness? Would he see all the good and bad and in between? All in an instant?

From the corner of his eye he saw movement – the attack was at hand. A spark of light, or what he thought was a spark of light, took him off guard. He looked in the direction, expecting the bottom to fall out at any moment. Yet, the extraordinary happened. Small dots of light began to appear one after the other. At first, it seemed like fireflies bobbing and darting among the cedars and pines, the birches and maples. Iridescent specs quickly expanded into larger bulbs to the point that there were hundreds forming in the forest. Spinning and swirling, the lights increased in size, merging and growing into larger beacons of brightness. They moved closer, and as they closed in, Moss saw that they were torches. Voices began to fill the wood. Shadowy figures began to move under the torches, grasping them firmly, carrying them directly toward where he stood. From the shadows came people, men and women moving with a purpose. At the head was an older man, gray-haired and balding, dressed in black except for a starched white collar. He held a Bible firmly in his grasp. A preacher, Moss thought. Walking with determination the preacher shouted, "She shall be cleansed and enter the Kingdom." That was followed by a cry, a plea, from somewhere within the center of the crowd. "No, please let me go," he heard the voice of a young woman speak. "Ignore her," the preacher ordered his flock, and they obeyed. Moss was stunned by the spectacle. The crowd seemed mesmerized and moved from the forest onto the path, its luster and radiance now dulled to pale gray. The torch lights burned steel blue, reflecting eerily on the crowd's expressionless faces. "What's wrong with you people?" he shouted out excited. "What the hell are you doing?" No one paid attention or gave notice to him. He may as well have been a ghost walking among them. The procession was almost upon him when the preacher raised his Bible high above his head. On cue, the crowd began to chant the Lord's Prayer over the pleas of the woman. "Our Father, who art in heaven …" Moss shouted for them to stop – to reason with them – to help the woman. But they continued to ignore him, reciting in a monotone, "… on earth as it is in heaven …"

The preacher lowered his Bible as he walked up to Moss. A sinister smile spread across his face as he continued to pray. There was intensity and madness in the preacher's gaze. He blinked purposefully. The window to his soul opened and Moss fell in. He saw a blackish pool, steaming and bubbling. He saw demons, deformed and decrepit, whispering and prowling along the pool's edge. He saw the preacher violating the innocent – his own child and those of his flock – and casting them into the pool. He saw the demons delight at the destruction of innocence – the torment, guilt, and shame. He saw the sinister smile of the preacher again as he stood before him. Raising his Bible, he pressed it on Moss's forehead and it passed directly through him. Moss felt icy tentacles gripping him, needling him, and slithering along his spine. One after the other, the entire procession passed through him, each piercing his soul like a hornet as each specter touched him – each sting toxic and venomous with hate and loathing. When she passed through him, amidst the mindless, emotionless chanting, her pleas struck him with a wave of soothing warmth, dousing him with relief. She and only she made eye contact, looking into his and begging for mercy. He stood and did nothing. Her arms were bound from behind. A rope was around her neck, another around her waist. Pulled and tugged, she choked and pleaded with her captors. As she passed through him, as the warmth embraced him, she looked upon

Moss and said calmly, "You'll never escape the Wailing Wood." Except it wasn't her voice, it was Pritchard's. With those words, the Lord's Prayer ended abruptly. The ghostly procession began to dissolve into shadowy forms – within moments reduced to the dance of a thousand fireflies. "She shall be cleansed," he heard echo one last time through the forest, "and enter the Kingdom."

The specs of light extinguished at once. Seconds later, from afar, atop the mountain, he heard a horrific, terrifying scream. The silence that followed was complete. Moss – stunned and shocked – collapsed to his knees, bowed his head, and sobbed uncontrollably. He had seen the innocent and the condemned. What men could do. What man did. "What have I done?" he bawled remorsefully. "I'll never get away with it. She'll get the insurance, and I'll hang." His mind's eye showed him bashing Pritchard. Laying him out by the fire. Making it look like an accident – just the way they'd planned it. He never saw it coming. "They never do," Louise had promised, and she was right. She, Pritchard's wife, did not blink an eye when she'd said it; only smiled, straddling him, naked.

IV

Moss continued to sob and moan and agonize until, pulling himself up, he found he was free to move. The forest around him had receded. The trail was free and clear; its luster and radiance gone. Regaining his composure, he began to run wildly down the winding path without caution or concern for what lay ahead. If he slipped or fell, he half expected to find himself in the clutches of the beasts, or the old men, or the preacher. Or perhaps devoured by the forest, or worse, back at that spot to confront the witch herself. He ran harder, scared to look back. It seemed like he'd been entombed there for days when miraculously he broke free to the other side. He had escaped the Wailing Wood and its enchantment – her enchantment. Stumbling across the field, hooting and yelling with delight, he made it to the embankment, jumped a stonewall, and rolled down onto the road. Laying on his back, looking at the gray sky, the beginning of a new day, a wave of relief came over him. He laughed out loud. He had survived the night.

Moss laid there laughing and whooping with delight for several minutes. "I've beaten the bitch," he thought. Lying there content, he sang out, "Ding-dong the witch is dead ...," when a voice asked, "Are you all right, dear?" Startled, Moss glanced around quickly. Fear rushed over him. For a split second, he was afraid he was back in the middle of the forest. He was about to yell, "Who's there?" when he spied an elderly woman standing in the road. She was bundled up against the cold in layers of shawls, wrapped snugly around her head and body. Her nose was red and runny. It seemed obvious to him that she had been standing there for several minutes. "Are you okay?" she asked.

Assured of his surroundings, he realized he was a mess, but was more surprised to see someone on the road this early, let alone an old woman. "I was lost, that's all," he said, finally. "I'm relieved I found my way out."

"Those woods are haunted, you know," she laughed lightly.

Moss feigned a smile. "So I've seen. If only I'd known that before I got lost in 'em, I could have avoided 'em all together."

She laughed again. "Ah, if everybody knew where they were going, they would never get lost," she said with the understanding of a sage.

"Well, I never want to get lost in there again," Moss said.

"It's okay to get lost from time to time," she replied in the same manner, "as long as you can find your way home."

Moss, annoyed at her pretension, thought about what he'd just gone through – the phantoms, the beasts, the preacher, the captive woman – about Pritchard and the money, about Louise, and said, "You never want to get lost in those woods, lady." He got up on one knee, then stood up slowly, covered in snow. His cheeks were still damp from the tears. Snot dripped from his nose. He wiped his face across the back of his sleeve. "Once you start down that path, or any path for that matter, there's no turning back," he added with an edge.

Without a word, she started off, walking toward town. She had a slight limp but moved quickly. Moss stood there for several moments,

watching her back, and wondering if he should let her go on alone –
but he thought better of it. If she was going into town, she'd provide a
nice distraction for the chief when he arrived and told him the bad
news. "Hey lady, wait up," he hollered, catching up to her. "I didn't
mean to offend you," he said. "I just went through hell in those woods."

"I'm not offended, believe me," she replied curtly.

"What are you doing out here alone at this hour?" he asked to
change the subject.

"Taking care of business," she answered. "Family business."

"Out here?" Moss asked. "Near these woods?"

"Yes," she answered. "This is my home. I am bound to this road,
those woods, this land, as surely as you are to your land, your home."

"I didn't mean anything by it," he said. She stopped and looked at
him with a blank expression but did not speak. "Honestly, I'm happy
to have your company," he said uneasily. "I just think a woman such as
yourself should not be out here alone."

"I really don't think of it as being alone, young man," she replied,
staring hard into Moss's eyes. "Those woods and this road have served
me well my whole life. I've never felt alone or lost here. In fact, I feel
quite content." She pulled at her shawl, wrapping it tightly around her,
sealing herself from a short burst of wind that sent snowflakes whirling
around her head.

"Who's going to protect you out here if something happens?" he
asked. The wind kicked up on his words. Snow, which had nearly
stopped, burst anew in intensity.

"Who's going to protect me?" she cackled loudly, raising her hand
and pointing a gnarly finger in his face. "Who's going to protect you?"
she added, as though scolding him. "You may want to consider that."
The wind and snow tapered as suddenly as it began. Moss swallowed
hard. His mouth went dry. He felt a pit grow in his stomach. That got
his attention, when it happened, when the weather died off, at the same
moment she lowered her hand from his face.

Moss stood there considering the possibility. "I don't know who's
going to protect either one of us, I guess," he said timidly. "All I meant

was the weather's bad enough on days like this. If you slipped and fell you could catch your death, let alone the wild animals around here, being stalked by something."

"Catch my death?" she laughed and shook her head as though it were the most fantastic thing she'd ever heard. "In these times, there's more to fear than wind and cold, or beasts abounding," she added, her voice rising in pitch and intensity.

"What more is there?" he blurted out impulsively.

She laughed under her breath and shook her head gleefully. "Why, man," she cried out loudly. "You should know that more than I!" she roared, extending her arms out and raising her hands up. A burst of wind and snow responded. The trees along the road swayed and shook, bowing to her command. A funnel of snow encompassed them. "Is there any creature more dangerous?" she yelled, standing like a preacher before a congregation. As she held her arms high, the funnel tightened around them. The wind pressure heightened. The force was so great, a vacuum pulled his lungs to the point of collapse. "Who but man would stand idly by and ignore the pleas of the innocent?" Whereupon she flicked her hands imperceptibly and lowered her arms. The wind ceased. The trees went still. The snow came to a halt. Her church – the earth, the elements – stood at rapt attention. He fell to a knee, winded, and took a long, deep breath. She looked down upon him in contempt and fury. Staring directly into Moss's eyes, she said, just above a whisper, "Is there any creature but man more capable of turning on his own kind?"

"Who – what – are you?" he asked in disbelief, her eyes fixed on his. "This can't be real."

"Oh, it's very real," she replied, her tone ominous and foreboding. "I am all that you are not. And you are mine now."

Moss stood up, unable to free himself from her gaze. When she finally blinked the windows to her soul opened, and Moss fell in. Tumbling and spinning, he landed hard into the pit, near the blackened pool, steaming and bubbling, and saw the faces of the fallen, begging for mercy. He saw the hunters, the preacher, the flock of lost souls, all were there, burning and bobbing in the pool. He saw the wolf-creatures prowling along the edge of the water, standing upright and growling ferociously at anyone who came near. He saw demons, hideous and deformed, laughing with satisfaction. They spit streams of thick, darkened venom at the damned, which struck them like jets of acid and made them cry out in agony. He saw a young woman appear – beautiful, voluptuous, and starkly naked – walking toward him. The beasts and the demons cowed submissively as she passed them, all the while ignoring the pleas of forgiveness from the pool. Dark curls of hair flowed over her shoulders, wrapping invitingly around her full breasts and aureoles. She approached Moss. Her hips swayed seductively. Slowly she came into focus – the captive – the woman from the forest. When she was close enough to touch he jolted. "Louise?" he said. She smiled at him, caressed his cheek with the palm of her hand. He relaxed at the touch, swaying gently; his head rolled back, his eyes shut involuntarily.

The force of the blow sent him staggering. He found himself face up in the snow, his lip bleeding and a welt across his face. The young Minerva stood over him, wrapped in shawls. A rope hung from her neck, another was draped around her waist. Her body was twisted and contorted, her neck was badly broken and her head hung limp. She turned and started off toward town. Her limp was pronounced, as the old woman's was before, but she walked even faster. Moss, angered, got up and ran at her. "You bitch!" he screamed, running hard. He grabbed her, spun her around to strike her, but facing him was Pritchard. His head was cracked open, dented badly and bleeding from the center of his forehead. Brain tissue protruded. Dozens of carrion flies swarmed and feasted around the fresh wound. Moss froze in horror, one hand raised in a fist, the other clinging to Pritchard's shoulder. "I warned you, you lying, cheating bastard," Pritchard said, and then smiled with satisfaction. "You'll never escape the Wailing Wood."

Moss teetered on the brink. Screaming hysterically, he yelled out, "No! No! No! I killed you, motherfucker!" Pritchard, ghastly and terrifying, stood there laughing with menace. Lunging for the specter's throat, Moss found no purchase, and simply passed through him, falling and falling and falling. He could hear the cackling laughter of Howlin' Minnie in his ear. Hornets by the thousands attacked and swarmed him as he tumbled recklessly, thwarting them futilely. They stung him and stabbed him relentlessly, forcing their way in. What he couldn't swallow entered him from behind. Buzzing rattled his brain. Hornets pierced the back of his eyeballs. Ferociously they penetrated his cavity, stinging and burrowing through his intestines. Downward he continued, into the pit of damned souls, into the blackened pool, and beyond. His lungs and veins filled with black oily, burning liquid, fetid and putrid. Passing into darkness, spinning and falling, hearing voices call out in agony, shouting and screaming for him. Heads and faces of creatures, grotesque and monstrous, rushed at him, snapping viciously, tearing his flesh as they passed. Battered and beaten, his lungs boiling, he continued to fall. He fell through the darkness and out into the world, passed the precipice of Parson's Drop, and slammed into the maple tree – her tree. Impaled atop the highest crown, convulsing and writhing, while black, molten liquid and hornets poured from his wound and mouth. Wanting nothing but death to consume him, he felt the tree release him, flicking him afar, and he continued to fall. Then and there, all his life passed before him, the treachery and deceit, the betrayal and murder, the terror of the Wailing Wood and the full comprehension of damnation – his very own – to walk down that forest path for all eternity, over and over. He struck the ground forcefully, gasping for his breath, his awareness seeping from him rapidly as he slipped further into the void, bewitched and bewildered. Rolling in the snow, he fought desperately to remember. He saw himself fall and fall and fall, again and again and again; faster, swifter, each time slammed harder into the ground.

He pulled himself up out of the snow and then dropped over face first, exhausted. His last thoughts grappled with memory, terrified and haunted. Running away – but from what? Awaking from a nightmare – from a consciousness without recollection. Thinking about what had just happened – if there was any other way back. He was so tired and cold – he knew he had to keep moving – or maybe burrow into the snow even deeper. Forget about everything. "What was the possibility of that?" he asked himself. Slim to none – he'd have a better chance of landing in hell. "What should I do?" he said aloud.

V

Confusion overwhelmed him like a wary traveler, lost and alone, standing at a crossroad. He was face-down in a snowdrift and came up with a bloody lip and a welt across his face. Cursing, he wondered how many times he'd fallen. He'd lost track. The night had been a long one, and it took all his strength to pick himself up. Moon rays broke through the clouds and over his shoulder, reflecting off the fresh snowfall, dotting pale, bluish sparkles on the broad, rolling field where he stood. The luster offered bare definition to the dark forest that bordered the field. He took a step in that direction and paused. A coyote sang out suddenly, eerily, from up on the mountain, sending a shiver of fright through him. A foreboding gripped him, but he quickly shook it off. He took a deep breath and continued. Dawn had to be approaching, he reckoned. Maybe an hour, more or less, till the safety of daylight, but he was unsure. Time eluded him.

Visiting an elderly neighbor on Christmas Eve, a young woman learns that she bears a special gift that is the key to her neighbor's salvation, and that of many other souls held captive by a monstrous evil.

Reflections of Mr. Ivy

When I was a child we lived in a neighborhood along Grove Street, right off the Kennebec Road going toward Duck's Head Pond. Ours was the fifth house on the left – number eleven. Mother's favorite number since she was a little girl. Eleven was my mother's age when Mrs. Somerset, my grandmother's best friend and reputed seer, told my mother that one day she would marry a man whose name began with the letter *P*, and that her first child would be a girl whom she must name Lilith. The seer told mother it was an important name because the child would need protection in her life, and the name would ward off the spirits of darkness and shadows. Otherwise, with a different name, she said, the child would be prone to their forces and temptation. Mrs. Somerset told all that to my mother right out of the blue. That's how she worked – how *it* worked. She could be sitting there one moment having a cigarette and a cup of coffee with Gram and the next she would be predicting something with uncanny accuracy. Mostly, she would delve into the forces-of-darkness thing, which tended to unnerve a heck of a lot of people. It was so unnatural to begin with – having this other sight – but to have it tuned in primarily to the dark side, well, you understand.

Years later my mother met a man named Kyle Reddy and she fell in love with him – or was falling in love with him. One evening when they were together she laughed when she recalled the part of the fortune Mrs. Somerset had foretold about my mother marrying a man whose name began with the letter *P*. Kyle smiled when she told him, but didn't say much, not till a few days later when he made his confession to her. He loved her and wanted to marry her, he said, but first he had two things he must tell her. The first was that he was under an obligation to name his first male child after himself, which was no problem at all for mother. What was the second thing, she asked? That the boy's name would be Percival Kyle Reddy IV, he told her. This, as you might expect, sent mother into a tizzy for a good, long spell. Kyle took her reaction as a refusal, and braced for his heart to be broken. But when mother regained her composure – for she had by then recalled the other half of what Mrs. Somerset had foretold – she looked into Kyle's eyes and said, that's okay with me, dearie, meaning his namesake and all, as long as you're okay with naming our first child, who will be a girl, Lilith. Kyle, I mean, my father, was overjoyed and greatly relieved – and he promised he'd never hold anything back from her again. My father never did ask my mother why my name had to be Lilith – maybe because he was so relieved that she'd agreed to marry him, or maybe because he was even more relieved when their first born turned out to be a daughter, not a son whom my mother would have wanted to name Lilith.

My parents often joked about how fate and Mrs. Somerset conspired to bring them together, and how fortunate they were with their special little girl, meaning me, of course.

I for one couldn't have been happier growing up in our neighborhood. Up and down the street children filled the houses – old capes and New Englanders – in every house but one. Number Thirteen Grove Street, our next door neighbor's house, set in from the road by a good fifty feet or more. I can remember the first time I saw the old man in the window of that house. I think I was four or five. Dressed in his peculiar, old fashioned black suit and wearing a bowler hat on his big head. He tipped his hat at me. Grinning broadly, he waved, and then beckoned for me to come. I kept walking past without responding, forbidden as I was from speaking to strangers. Though the fact of the matter was he wasn't saying anything to me because he was inside and I was outside, and I couldn't really call him a stranger because, after all, he was our neighbor. His house was a mansion compared to all the other houses on the street – compared to most of the houses in town. My father said it was an example of high Victorian architecture and was once one of the grandest houses in the county. For years I thought every run down, ramshackle big house I saw was an example of high Victorian architecture. To me and the rest of the children in the neighborhood, the mansion looked out of place among all the other modest-sized houses on our street.

The family that lived there was rarely seen. They were what my parents called recluses. They were an old family who'd been in town for generations. My father said they went by the name of Dalrymple. But I called the old fashioned man in the window Mr. Ivy because of all the ivy plants that grew over the side of the house and wrapped around the porch. As time went by, he greeted me occasionally, always standing in the window, grinning ear-to-ear, cheerfully tipping his hat. From time to time he would beckon to me, but I always remembered what my parents told me. There was no rhyme or reason to when I'd see him, either. Sometimes it was when I went to school or came back from playing with the many children who lived on the street. I never saw him in his yard or even sitting on the porch, but only through the window.

My two best friends growing up were Elissa Bayley Seton and Joan D'arc. They called me Lilith of the Garden. My mother laughed with delight at me and referred to my two friends as little saints. One afternoon when returning from the playground we passed the Dalrymple's old mansion. Mr. Ivy was there. He waved and tipped his hat as he normally did, but his smile turned to a grimace unexpectedly. Elissa Bayley Seton and Joan D'arc, whose backs were turned to the house, saw me wave and looked. They asked me who I was waving to and I told them Mr. Ivy. They turned to look again but Mr. Ivy had departed. I noticed the concern on both of my friends faces, but it quickly passed. Their familiar smiles broke across their faces again. I said he waves to me from inside the house, standing in that window. Elissa Bayley Seton said her father told her never to go near the house. Joan D'arc's father said it was a shame, what had happened to the family, how they had fallen, but people make their own choices. Funny how it was, I told them, I never see the family at all, other than Mr. Ivy from time to time. We continued on our way and spoke no more of it.

Later that night I asked my mother about the family next door. She answered, ever cheerful, that the house was in pretty much the same condition when she was a girl. The family never bothered with anyone, my mother said, so in return, no one ever bothered with them. They were to be left to their own devices. A shame, really, how people choose to live their lives. I told her about Mr. Ivy and she listened intently, but said nothing. She seemed concerned, as my friends Elissa Bayley Seton and Joan D'arc had been, but her warm smile soon returned. She told me not to fret about Mr. Ivy, to ignore him and he'd go away.

My mother and father always treated me differently. Not that they favored me above my two brothers and younger sister when they came along. I supposed, once my mother took to what Mrs. Somerset had said, she and my father thought of me as special. For them I was like a present they waited all year long to open on Christmas day, which they did, because that was the day that I was born.

When I was eight years old my grandmother gave me a camera for Christmas – and as a birthday present too, because they were the same day. I loved the camera very much. My grandmother taught me how to use it – how to take pictures certain ways, depending on the light, and how to have the film in the camera developed. I took the camera with me wherever I went. It was as special to me as my grandmother.

Gram was a professional photographer, famed for her black and white portraits. My mother told me that art critics loved Gram's pictures because she captured the true identities of people. We went down to Boston once to view an exhibit of her work. There were lots of her pictures hanging in a special wing of a gallery. I remember that my mother and father were very proud. Many people came up to them that day to say how special grandmother and her pictures were. We were there for hours. As we walked from picture to picture, my grandmother told a story behind each person she had photographed. I was too young and bored to understand. When we approached the last picture in the exhibit my grandmother made me cover my eyes and promise not to open them until she told me to. When she did, I dropped my hands from my face and couldn't believe what I saw. It was a picture of me. I looked very happy and peaceful, staring directly into the lens. My mother and father said it was incredible and unbelievable, and asked my grandmother how she did it. She said it wasn't her. The camera did all the work. My grandmother held me close and said that picture caught the true essence of who I am. Mother and father got all teary-eyed, which I couldn't understand because I looked so happy in the picture, not sad. My grandmother smiled at me, looked at the picture with admiration, and said I was radiant. Everyone who went by also said I was radiant. I wasn't sure what they meant, but I supposed it was because of the whitish glow that surrounded the top of my head in the picture. My grandmother said it was my aura. At the time I asked what "her yora" was and it made her laugh. I loved my grandmother. She treated me special, too.

I was twelve when my grandmother died. At the gravesite during her funeral there were so many people I lost count. She had many friends and was well-liked and loved by people far and wide. I remember wishing that I would touch that many people in my life someday. I brought my camera to the service. I thought Gram would have wanted it that way. It seemed odd in a morbid way to do such a thing – take pictures of people while they grieved – but grandmother and I had always taken pictures together. We spent hours scrapbooking them into albums. As grandmother was lowered into the ground I began to snap pictures all around me. I, too, wanted to capture the essence of all those who were at the service.

A few weeks after the funeral I showed my mother and father the album I made of the graveside service. There were so many finely dressed people in it, some who did not seem at all sad and others who were very sad. After my mother opened the album she cupped her hand to her mouth and began to cry. My father moaned and asked me for my camera. I told him no, that grandmother would have wanted me to take those pictures. He simply looked at me and said, "Lilith," the way he always sounded when he was serious. I handed my father the camera. They took the album from me too, which upset me terribly. I went to my room and cried, not knowing what I had done that was so wrong.

Later that night as I lay in my bed, I heard my parents speaking from their bedroom. I decided to have my say. I crept down the hallway but stopped short at their doorway when my mother, still sobbing, said to my father, "Kyle, that's them. They're all here in the pictures. My God, they were all there at the funeral! Aunt Martha, Aunt Catherine, Uncle Henry, Nanny Walters, Papa Walters, Uncle James, Cousin Bess, Cousin Richard, Uncle Wes ..." My mother went on naming people I had heard mention of but never met. My father kept reassuring her it would be all right, that maybe it was old film in the camera. And mother replied, "Please, Kyle! That was Mrs. Somerset standing there smiling right into the camera, waving. How could that be all right?"

Quietly I went back to my room. For the rest of the night I lay in my bed, in the dark, thinking. I tossed and turned. I cried some more, too. I thought about all the names mother had said – strangers, but familiar in an odd way. Mostly, I couldn't get the name of Mrs. Somerset out of my head. Mother and grandmother had spoken of her so often. She had been an inspiration and was dearly missed these many years past.

The next day I talked to my friends Elissa Bayley Seton and Joan D'arc, who met me outside of my house every morning to walk with me to school or wherever else I was going. I told them how upset mother and father had been. Elissa Bayley Seton said that they would get over things and be okay in the weeks to come. My grandmother's spirit passed through me and lived on. Her father had told her that's how it worked. She said that my parents would come to understand that in time. Joan D'arc said that what Elissa Bayley Seton had told me was true, how my grandmother's spirit shined bright in me. How I would always be drawn to the light, but more importantly, how the light would always be drawn to me. She said that her father had told her to tell me that. My friends always said the right things to me, ever since I first met them as a little girl, right outside my house. It was as though they carried me through my dark hours.

In the days, weeks, and months that followed, I said nothing to my parents about what I had overheard. Mother and father chose not to speak of that evening to me, either. But one day they gave my camera back to me and apologized for taking it. I never did see the album again. Not that it mattered. I had the negatives, which I kept to myself. My parents never asked for them and I never spoke of them. Out of respect for my parents, my mother especially, I stored them away deep in my bedroom closet. I kept the memories stored deep inside of myself, too, all but forgetting them.

When I was starting high school my good friends Elissa Bayley Seton and Joan D'arc moved away. First, Elissa Bayley Seton went, saying her father had work elsewhere to attend to, and that the family was leaving. Then, a short time later Joan D'arc left. She told me that she was going to boarding school. Her father said it was time for her to spread her wings. She had accomplished all she could here in the Lost Kingdom of Moose Harbor. I cried when they left. I had known them so long it was as though they were a part of me. I moped around the house for weeks afterward, sobbing occasionally.

One day my mother asked me why I was so sad. I told her that I couldn't get over my best friends leaving. She smiled and gave me a big, warm hug. She said my little saints, which is what she always had called them, had not gone far. She told me it would be all right; that friends never really leave but pass all they have that's good in them through their friends and live on. All those memories I had buried in me in the days after my grandmother died came bubbling up. I remembered how my parents reacted when they opened the photo album of the graveside service. I especially remembered what Elissa Bayley Seton and Joan D'arc had said. I realized then and there that I, too, would come to understand.

As the years went by and I grew, I often thought of all the wonderful and meaningful experiences that made me who I am. I would see Mr. Ivy occasionally, too, standing in the window, seemingly ageless, tipping his bowler hat, waving and smiling, and motioning me to come in. After seeing Mr. Ivy so many years in the window inviting me in, I decided to go introduce myself. I was a woman now. It was Christmas Eve and I was turning twenty-one the very next day. I had never been afraid of Mr. Ivy, not even as a little girl. In all the years he had waved at me he had never left the house. I had never spoken to him, asked him why he never came outside, or why he wore the same clothes every day. I had never been that curious, to be honest. I had respected what my parents had told me about the Dalrymples. I had respected their privacy and left them alone to their own devices.

I don't know what came over me that day, however. Maybe it was the spirit of Christmastime, which I carried with me all the time, each day, because it was such a big part of me. I was on my way home from a walk when I passed number Thirteen Grove Street. I glanced over and saw Mr. Ivy tipping his hat in the window. His smile was especially warm and inviting. Impulsively, I turned down the Dalrymple's walkway, deciding to finally introduce myself and wish him a merry Christmas. I walked right up to the door and knocked. I waited and waited, expecting Mr. Ivy to come running to the door and greet me as an old friend. I knocked again, waiting patiently. Still no one came to the door. I was puzzled, but then I thought that maybe he was shy and embarrassed. So many years had passed since the first time he had invited me in, that now, maybe he didn't know what to do on the day I accepted his invitation. I laughed and knocked one last time, and waited another minute. Still no one came, which made me feel suddenly embarrassed, about not respecting people's privacy and leaving them to their own devices. But when I turned to leave the door opened partially. I stood there amazed – I have to say – looking into the eyes of a short, bent man. His hair was snowy and wavy. His arms hung to his knees. I noticed his hands shook slightly. His fingers were long and bony. There were wrinkles spreading from the corners of his mouth that curled up when he said, "Hello." I had never seen anyone that old, and I am not proud to admit it, but I was speechless. "Can I help you?" he asked politely.

After another moment or two, I stammered out, "Excuse me, sir, I came to see Mr. Ivy."

The man looked perplexed, and then said, "There is no one here by that name, young lady." He began to close the door slowly.

"Excuse me, sir," I said.

"Yes," he said, holding the door.

"What I meant was – I came to see the man in the window – to wish him a merry Christmas. I've seen him there forever, and he always waves at me. I just wanted to say, 'hi.'"

Once more he looked at me perplexed. "Young lady, I am very old and it's very cold. Have yourself a merry Christmas." He began to close the door again.

"But sir," I said, being persistent. "There was a man in the window!"

He held the door, hesitating. A draft rushed out from the hallway abruptly, from nowhere, and collided with me. The chill stung me. "You should come inside," he said, wearily. "It's too cold."

"I shouldn't impose," I replied, suddenly afraid.

"You must," he answered, "or he'll never leave you or me alone."

I followed him in and shut the door behind me. Everything about the place seemed old and musty. The Dalrymple house seemed from another time and place. There were gas lamps, an old wood stove, and furniture covered in velvet. I couldn't help but think of the pictures my grandmother had showed me years before. The ones of her and Mrs. Somerset as little girls, sitting prim and proper in strange clothes on a sofa like the one I was being led to. I followed the old man into a room he called a parlor. I quickly recognized the window. This was the room. That window was where Mr. Ivy always stood. That was what I told the old, bent man. He said that Mr. Ivy was not here. But from that window the old man himself had watched me walk by my whole life. "I've seen you just about every day from the time you could walk. At times I wanted to scream out for you to run. How close – so many times – he nearly had you."

He went on to say that he could see everything about me, and told me I had a strong aura. That made me smile, bringing back the memories of my grandmother's exhibit. He excused himself for being so rude and introduced himself as Mr. Dalrymple. You are Lilith of the Garden, he said to me. He knew that was what my two dearest friends had called me. He had heard them say it so many times that it was the only name he knew me by. Then he asked me to stand in the window and asked me what I saw, which I did. I saw nothing but the walkway I had come up, the street, the snow banks rolled up along the driveways and road, and good old Mr. Taylor walking his German Shepherd, Bullet. This was what I said to the old, bent man. The old man said that was what he saw, too, because I was inside with him. "You are a very special child, Lilith of the Garden," he said. "We have waited for you such a long, long time." I thought it rude to ask who he was including when he said "we," seeing there was only he and I.

We were standing next to each other in the window, looking out at the street, silently, for a long time. Just as I thought the moment awkward, that perhaps I'd overstayed my welcome, and was about to excuse myself and leave, he said, "There was a man named Hamilton Browne who once lived here in Downeast Way. He made a fortune in sawmills – owned a dozen throughout the state. He lived alone up on Scammon Ridge in a large mansion. I hear that house is but a shell now, though I really wouldn't know. Hamilton made so much money cutting lumber he built libraries in each one of the towns where he had a mill. Everyone considered him a model citizen. There was talk at one time of a run for governor.

"My father had his own business here in town, a small hardware store that my grandfather had started. My father was well-known and well-liked, and much respected here in the community as an honest businessman. The business thrived and we lived very comfortably. One day my father got a good bargain on lumber and bought several pallets, never thinking twice about it. Turns out the lumber came from a rival of Hamilton Browne. The very next day he burst into my father's store, Hamilton did, and cursed my father in front of all the customers. Told him then and there he was going to ruin my father.

"My father only scratched his head, but the funny thing was, in a short time, the banks stopped my father's credit line for the business. Vendors began demanding payment in full upon delivery. Then another hardware store opened across town. When you're going through it, my father used to say, you don't really know what's happening until it's too late. You simply can't believe it's happening until it's too late. He lost the business eighty years ago today. Christmas Eve my father shut it up

73

for good. I was a boy, ten years old, and my sister Mildred was eight. The Depression hit the following year, and believe me, we struggled. My father turned to the sea, started fishing, and occasionally running the rum for old man Huxley, and my mother became a laundress.

"It happened when my father was gone to sea. My mother took the job at the Browne Mansion. She didn't want to because she hated the man. But the Depression was a powerful thing. It crushed a lot of people. It robbed them of their dignity. When you lose your dignity you'll do just about anything to survive. Anything is better than nothing. We owned our house, thankfully, but were living week to week, and were already missing more than one meal a day.

"It turns out that Hamilton Browne loved my mother – always had from the first time he'd walked into the store in 1916. That was what all the pain and suffering he'd caused our family was about. Jealousy and envy. Her first day on the job at his mansion, he told my mother he was a self-made man, and could buy and sell men like my father who had no future at all. He said it was time she came to her senses and moved in with him. She slapped his face and he laughed. Then he forced himself upon her, and for all intents and purposes, raped her. When he was finished he said he wanted to give her something to remember him by, and laughed again. He opened his wallet and produced five-thousand dollars cash. She slapped his face again, and then took the money. Hamilton Browne again laughed, long and hard. He said he'd always be there watching over her, her and her family, and now they'd never escape him because they'd been bought. He'd be waiting there each and every day to collect his money in flesh. He'd greet them each day from the threshold of hell, and take every one of them with him – just like all the others who dared challenge him – straight to hell. My mother slapped his face one more time and left.

"That night Hamilton Browne put on his finest suit and dress hat, and walked right into one of his sawmills, the one up on Pratt Road – it's still there, I hear, abandoned now, or so I'm told. He, Hamilton Browne, went into that mill and walked head first into a circular saw the size of a small Ferris wheel. He left a note behind confessing to all

74

– what he'd done to my mother, but other women, too. Younger women – anonymous women from the working classes – left on their own to survive – who were not as lucky as my mother and had disappeared without a trace. They found them all out in back of the mansion planted under a willow tree. That's where they also found my father. He had not made it to sea his last time out. Hamilton Browne had murdered him after my father refused an offer of five-thousand dollars to buy him out – to buy my mother.

"Shortly thereafter he came as he said he would – to collect.

"My mother was distraught – we all were – as you can imagine. Time passed, day in and day out, week after week, and soon the months rolled by into years. My mother had a friend – someone you know who told me all about you – who came to help in the only way she could. She kept him at bay, but that was all she could do. One day, my aunt came to visit. My mother said she'd be right back, and then gave my sister and me a big hug, and began to weep sadly. She went out the door and down the walkway – the same one you came up – went all the way to the street and stopped. My mother seemed to take a deep breath. She looked back at me and my sister and my aunt one last time and blew us a kiss, smiling lovingly. Behind her he appeared in his suit and hat, smiling and waving at us. He tipped his hat, and then my mother stepped onto Grove Street and disappeared before our eyes. We never saw her again.

"It's never changed, either. He's out there always, waiting for us – well, me now, I'm the last one. If I fall, my family and all the others will be trapped with him for eternity. He's kept us imprisoned here all these years in our own hell, anyway. My mother's friend, Gladys Somerset, Mrs. Somerset to you, did what she could – pushed him out to the middle of the street. He's never been able to get closer.

"In the last years of her life Mrs. Somerset would frequently visit my sister and me to reassure us. One day, she said, a young girl would arrive. Kind and innocent, she could send him away to the hell that awaits him. More importantly, she will free all those he has imprisoned, including your mother and father. She alone, the girl, could do this, but she alone must discover how on her own terms. In the simplest of ways, like the turn of the tide, she could prevail. You, my child, are that girl. You don't know how I've longed to call you – each and every time you stopped to look at him – Mr. Ivy."

I was petrified. For the first time in my life I was at odds with who I am. I knew I was special – in a way. I couldn't deny it further. All that had happened around me growing up was proof enough. I thanked Mr. Dalrymple. I wished him a merry Christmas and excused myself – as much as I could – because I was falling to pieces. At the door he grasped my arm. I thought for a moment he was not going to let me leave. His bony fingers clenched me firmly. He looked me right in my eyes. I saw all the loss and despair, the promise and longing, the kindness and compassion – and the unfathomable hope that he and his family would one day be free of this terrible curse.

"I believe in you," he said, smiling, and dropped a single tear, then released me.

I was quite overwhelmed by the moment and embraced him – a man I had not known in all my years, my next door neighbor, yet somehow, someway, a man I had been intricately connected to. Tearfully, I wished him a merry Christmas, again, and then he said happy birthday to me, which took me aback. The look on my face must have been revealing, for he said that Mrs. Somerset had told them they'd know who the girl was – he and his sister – for she'd be born on Christmas Day.

The following morning, Christmas Day, my twenty-first birthday, was my most special day. I had arrived home from Mr. Dalrymple's a mess the evening before. Even though it was Christmas Eve, mother and father had given me the space I needed. After so many years they knew better than to ask. I was having a special moment. I recovered in a short time and celebrated that evening with my family. The next morning I received a gift – a new camera – from mother and father. It was a modern digital camera, not an old-style film camera like the one my grandmother had given me years earlier. And also, wrapped in the same box, beneath the camera, was my old photo album from Gram's funeral. I got all blubbery. Mother got all blubbery. Even father got a little blubbery. Percival Kyle Reddy IV thought we were all nuts, which was okay. That's why we loved him. I took pictures of my family as they opened their presents. The camera had a big display on it, which allowed me to view the pictures as I took them. We sang Christmas carols along with Bing Crosby and laughed. None of the Reddy clan would be auditioning for the Saint Alphonzo choir anytime soon. It didn't matter to us. We were a happy family.

Later that morning I took my camera with me outside to take a few snapshots. The ground was covered in a fresh snowfall from the night before. I saw Mr. Taylor walking Bullet and wished them both a merry Christmas. Impulsively, I turned toward the Dalrymple house and waved. I knew the old man would be standing there so I mouthed merry Christmas to him, even though the only person I saw was Mr. Ivy, greeting me as he always had since I was a little girl. I raised my camera quickly and snapped several shots in succession.

As I reviewed the images on the camera's display screen, for the first time I saw Mr. Ivy as he truly was, his face flush with anger and rage, sinister and diabolical. Shadows danced around him. Behind him I could make out the heads and shoulders of what looked like, or what I guessed were, all the lost people – his captive souls. In each successive picture the shadows grew and his gaze became more terrifying. I looked at the images in the camera's display one at a time. After each I looked up again at him. He stood there smiling and waving with his hand for me to come in. When I came to the last picture I nearly dropped the camera in the snow. Standing between me and Mr. Ivy were my grandmother and Mrs. Somerset side by side. All the familiar faces were there too, the people I had never met but had seen in the pictures in the photo album from my grandmother's funeral. Most special to me was the appearance of Elissa Bayley Seton and Joan D'arc, their wings spread broadly, smiling at me as they always had. When I saw their faces I remembered how they had comforted me in my darkest hours. Yet today was not a dark day, not when I looked into the camera, at that last picture. Around me was a brilliant aura – a bright light. "The light," I said aloud. The realization struck me. "It's the light!" Finally,

I understood why I was special. How I could help all those poor, lost souls. How I could free Mr. Dalrymple. How I could send Mr. Ivy away – away to where he belonged – to banish him into darkness for all eternity. I looked up at the window, at Mr. Ivy as he smiled and waved, as he tipped his hat and beckoned graciously for me to come join him. In that moment I fully comprehended what it was I had to do that I had never done before. In that moment I looked at Mr. Ivy – directly in his eyes – and I turned around.

When Owen Dropped By

By the time Owen dropped by, the wind had finally calmed and the rain was letting up. We'd been expecting him for more than an hour, Owen and the other two wharf rats, Burgess and Lawrence. Owen was usually last to arrive, prone as he was to lose his way, forgetful and so easily sidetracked. That's why, when he walked into the study at Crawford's house, we were genuinely surprised. Not only because he was first to arrive, ahead of Burgess and Lawrence who usually arrived on time, but also because we hadn't even heard him come in.

We were gathering to watch the ballgame, have a beer or two, and throw it at each other—the usual BS—like we did every Thursday night. Grilling was standard fair before the game, but not today. The rain had come in hard and sideways that afternoon, pelting the side of the house for about an hour. Where Crawford and I were sitting, facing a set of French windows, we could see out onto his backyard and beyond. As the wind tailed off, a fog had rolled in. We watched it curl around the hulls of boats moored out on the harbor. Wisps at first, like shapeless apparitions, eerie-like, restless and fleeting. But then the fog expanded and engulfed even the larger boats for moments or more. Playing tricks with the eyes, the fog made it seem as though the boats were moving through it as the fog passed through each boat.

Fog could do that to you, play tricks and stuff if you gawked at it long enough. After a few beers, while staring out at a fog, Owen would often say he was prone to 'hop'tical' illusions, which was good for a laugh. But he once claimed that he could see spirits of lost sailors drifting in the fog, trying to find their way to shore, which wasn't good for much. In fact, the only thing it was good for was a mood swing. Crawford later wondered out loud if it was time for an intervention, or if it was too late for that because the boy had completely gone off-kilter.

That's why when Owen entered the room it was not too weird to see him still dressed in his bibs and raincoat, especially since he was running late. Together Owen and Burgess and Lawrence trapped lobster by trade, and we figured they must have put in some time on the boat today even though the weather was crappy. In the summer, during soft-shell season, there was good money to be made, so they pushed it everyday. By the looks of him he must have just left the boat. Owen's hair was all wet, and rivulets of water dripped from him and his gear. Without taking off his coat, he quietly sat down opposite us in his usual roost, a rocking chair by the window, and began rocking slowly. I took a quick look-see down the hall for the other two, expecting them to follow, but he had arrived alone.

"What the hell kept you?" Crawford joked.

Owen didn't reply, but just stared down the hall like he was expecting the other boys to show up any second.

"Where's the other two? You guys ain't been running whores again down at the Cumberland House, have ya?"

Most times that was good for a laugh, but not tonight. Crawford's wife was within earshot, so we got an earful from the other room before we could even crack a smile.

"Damn you, Silas Crawford," she shouted. "Watch your tongue—at least *try* to set an example." Presumably, she was referring to an example for the grandkids, who were sitting with her two rooms over where she was supposedly watching TV. I'm guessing she must have been doing just that—watching TV, because she surely wasn't listening to it.

"What's on your mind, Vera?" Crawford shouted back. "'Cause I'm talkin' horses, damn it! I said horses, running the horses! As in harness racing! The trotters are running down at Cumberland right now! If you're gonna eavesdrop at least get it right." He rolled his eyes and grinned.

"Throw it all you want, Silas, but you better not be rolling those beady eyes of yours," she shouted.

I began to look around the room. "There a hidden camera, Crawford?" I whispered, wondering. "The Cumberland races aren't for another month," I added.

"Yea, but she doesn't know that," he said.

"Yes, I do," Vera shouted.

Crawford, his frustration rising, was about to throw it back, but his words were cut by a loud pounding at the front door, enough that it started us in our seats.

"I'll get it, Vera," Crawford shouted, and went down the front hallway muttering.

I turned back to Owen. "Must be Burgess and Lawrence," I said, throwing a thumb over my shoulder. I noticed a small puddle on the wooden floor beneath the rocker around his rubber boots. I pointed to it. "Say, Owen," I said, "Vera sees that you're gonna wish you were dead." He reached over, touched my wrist. Cold as it was, he cracked a hint of a smile that left me colder.

"What!" Crawford gave a shout. Owen leaned forward. I turned to look and then stood. There, in the doorway, was Burgess. He was out of breath and soaked, his coat dripping with water. He gestured anxiously to Crawford. He looked and motioned to me. Crawford was already reaching for his coat when I began to move that way.

"The mooring broke," I heard Burgess say as I approached them. "We had to get out there and get the boat before it ran aground."

"You should have called," Crawford said.

"We didn't have time. We were trying to beat the storm so we jury-rigged a small outboard to that old dory he has. We were nearly there, had nearly caught it, chuggin' along, when the fog rolled in! We had a clear view of his boat and then poof—swallowed by the fog." He was rambling and his hands jerked as he spoke. "A minute later we hear the whine of an engine. It's getting close. We give a shout but it's too late. It was a trawler out of Owls Head. He'd heard us, was turning, when the bow appeared through the fog and clipped the front of us. It plunged the back end of the dory under. We launched like a catapult into the dark water—icy as hell. I went under—damn—only God knows how far down, pulled under by the force of the dory and trawler I guess. I struggled, Crawford, I damn gave it everything and finally broke free. I kicked and stroked skyward with all I had. When I had nothing left to give I gave it that much more and broke the surface." He shook his head hard, like he was trying to shake the memory free. He began to sob and wiped his face with the palms of his hands.

I looked beyond him, outside, for Lawrence, but Burgess stood there alone. I swallowed hard, forming the question in my head—afraid of the answer—the one that anyone who works the sea fears to hear more than anything. Mid-August, on the Gulf of Maine, on the hottest days, the water is still bone-chilling cold. It's dark, too, even when the sun shines bright. But in a fog, that water takes on a darker shade of ink. You don't want to go down in those waters. If the cold doesn't get you, the darkness will.

"'We,' Burgess?" I finally asked. "You mean you and Lawrence?"

He looked at me oddly and began to speak, but stopped short, interrupted by flashing lights from a cop car that was bearing down the street toward us. It braked and pulled in out front. The next thing I knew Vera and grandkids came rumbling our way at the commotion and, crowded at the door, we all stared in anticipation, fearing for the worse.

The front door of the car pushed open, the passenger side. It was Lawrence who jumped out. "They found him," he cried out, and came running our way. Right up to the doorstep. Stopping before Burgess,

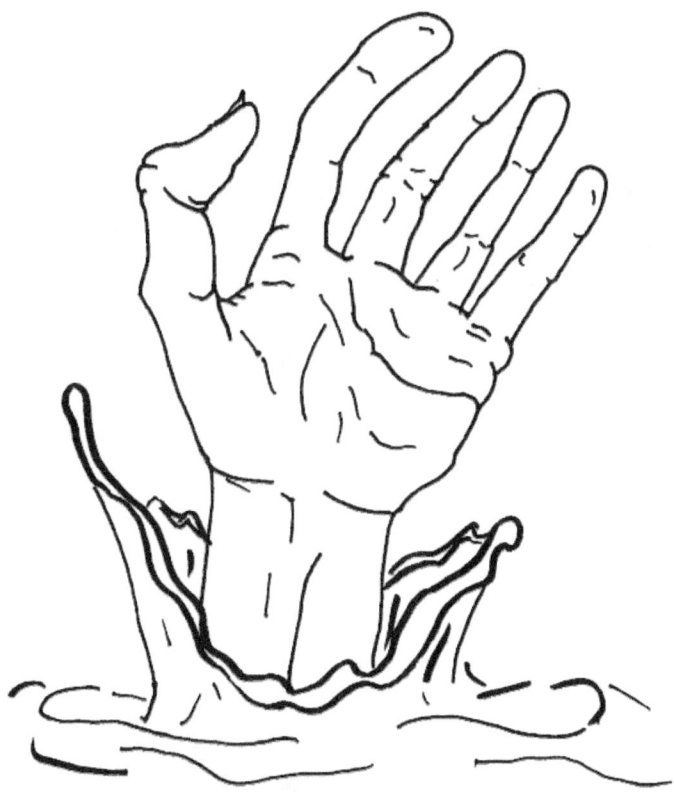

looking directly into his eyes, he tried to speak, but simply shook his head as he mouthed the words silently.

My eyes found Crawford's then; his face had turned ashen gray and I felt the blood drain from mine. We turned slowly, fearfully, our eyes staring down the hallway into the study. The rocking chair suddenly stilled. But for a puddle of water beneath the runners, the room was empty.

All these years later, I still shudder whenever I think of that day when Owen dropped by. Wonder how he had found his way to Crawford's? Hours after he had gone down in those dark, cold waters forever.

We never could talk that much about it, Crawford and I. Too much to think of, really, though sometimes I lay awake at night—restless and weary—as it plays out in my head and I wonder still. I see Owen sitting there in his bibs and raincoat, water dripping off him, rocking in silence. I want to ask him if he's okay, but I also want to ask him how—how he made it there to Crawford's—how he found his way out of the depth of the cold and dark water after he'd drowned.

These days, whenever a fog rolls in, sometimes I pause and stare out on the harbor. I don't see any lost sailors drifting there. No, I'm not that unhinged, just a little unhinged. Because I swear I can feel at least one of those sailors. At my wrist, an icy touch lands, like the one he left me with—and then I see that cold smile in my head. "Why me, Owen?" I ask aloud. "What in God's name do you want from me?"

But I hear no answer. I never do.

That day will come, I know, when I hear him. It's the only thing I'm sure of. Someday, Owen will have his say and I'll have my answer.

On a forsaken stretch of coastal road down east, a restless spectral soul is said to wander along an old bridge. For most it's just lore. But for one man, it's a story he'll never forget.

And Then There Were Three

"The old bridge to Moose Harbor?" the man behind the counter repeated my question thoughtfully, a second time, excepting the 'How do I find' part that began the question. I nodded thoughtfully, again, a second time, even with the guy on my right clearing his throat loudly, again, for a second time.

It had been ages since I had to stop to ask directions at a gas station. But I had lost my way and my cell phone reception an hour back, about the same time I had my epiphany: There's a reason why there is no cell phone reception when you're in the middle of nowhere. As a matter of fact, that's what makes it the middle of nowhere.

"Let me tell you a secret," he leaned in close over the counter and whispered. "You can't get there from here."

"You got me," I said, and forced a smile. The guy beside me rolled his eyes, "For the love of God, Harvey!"

"Sorry, it's been a long day," he said to me with a chuckle, then looked to the guy on my right. "Jeesum Crow, Dean, don't have a tizzy. I was just having a laugh."

"I'm not having a tizzy, and I'm not laughing, either. That's lame – plain and simple – like you."

"Don't mind him, mister. He works for the town, collects road kill. Mondays can be very tough on him."

I was tired, needed gas and directions, and yet, even though I knew I was going to hate myself for going there, I had to state the obvious. "But today is Sunday."

"And tomorrow is the first day of a long work week."

"Just tell him where to go, Harvey," said Dean. "So we can all get on with our lives."

"I'm gonna tell you where to go, Dean, if you keep throwing it."

"About Moose Harbor," I spoke up. "Please. I'm trying to find the old bridge." It didn't matter that I had been driving for hours to get here, after dark. I'd been traveling up and over and around the low mountains along the Maine coast – in search of the last vestiges of the Eastern Frontier that my boss had sold me on. There was a great story up here to follow, he had said, and he'd told me to persevere. So I persevered. A mix of work and pleasure and a bit intellectual curiosity had gotten me this far.

"Course you can get 'upta Moose Harbor from here," Harvey said calmly. "But you gotta go the long way."

"The long way?" I asked.

"Yupper! The new bridge over to Bean's Point isn't opened yet. You gotta drive 'upta the Narrows and over, then down."

"That's the only way? I thought there was a shortcut. When my phone had a signal I was certain there was a bridge near here. The bridge at gypsy something."

He hesitated, and said, "Yeah … but no."

"Dammit, Harvey," Dean interrupted and slammed a bill on the counter in front of the twenty I had laid down. "Put ten on pump number two – that would be the other pump, the one he's not using." He nodded at me. "Sorry, mister," he said, "I'm running late." My eyes followed him outside to the small gas pump island. His pickup truck was parked opposite my old Jeep four-door.

"He'll be okay," Harvey smiled. "He's got a lot to deal with tomorrow."

I was going to take him for his word about the bridge, but because of the way he had hesitated, I had to ask him, "Usually when they build a new bridge to replace an old bridge, they keep the old bridge open until the new bridge is ready. Isn't that what they usually do?"

"It 'tiz, but there is no bridge to Bean's Point right now. They're building it just down the road." He paused, began to speak but hesitated again, and then said, "Best to go the long way. It's a safer bet." He pulled a map from the display case below the countertop and opened it. "Four miles up that way and the road forks – bear left." He pointed at a spot on the map and then out the window to the road. "You'll bump into Route One another five miles after that. Turn right and you're on your way."

I sighed deeply, frustrated, feeling hosed.

"Sure it's longer – believe me, I know," he commiserated. "Too many moose in the roadway these days – been over a dozen accidents this summer alone – up on the way to – oh, it doesn't matter."

"Too many moose?" I laughed. I didn't mean to, but I did. "It does matter. It's too far south, isn't it, for moose around here?"

He shrugged and shook his head, no. "True, there's not as many moose as 'upta Piscataquis County, but there are still lots of 'em. Just two or three summers ago, down in Camden, a moose walked right into an office building in the middle of town."

"Well, where are the moose going to move to when the new bridge opens?" I asked. "Back up to Moosehead Lake?"

"Don't believe me. Ask Dean, he'll tell ya. That gas he's gettin' is for his chainsaw."

"Holy shit," I breathed, and finally relented. "All right, how much do I owe you?"

"Nothing for the directions, but the map's two dollars, plus the twenty for gas."

"I can live with that," I said and paid him, thinking I could have saved the last ten minutes of my life if I'd just bought the damn map in the first place.

At my car I lifted the nozzle and began pumping gas. My eye caught Dean's. He was standing next to a five-gallon gas can, looking at me.

"Psst," he said. "Where is it you going? Moose Harbor was it?"

I nodded. "Trying to, without having to drive another hour, or hit a moose."

"Hmm, yes, there have been a few collisions this summer." He picked up the gas can and placed it into the bed of his pickup – right next to a big old McCulloch chainsaw. In the pump island's bluish light I noticed bloodstains splattered up and down the length of the saw's long blade. "But that's not the reason he's steering you away from that bridge at Gypsy's Bluff."

"Oh, really," I said.

"Really," he repeated.

"There really is a bridge at gypsy something or other?"

"Indeed there really is."

"It's an odd name for these parts. You don't associate down east Maine with gypsies."

"No, you certainly don't, mister." He paused for a moment, looked me up and down. "You look like a good egg," he said. "Let me tell you a secret."

"Please, I just fell for that."

"Ha! No – that's not what I was going to say."

I raised a brow. "What then?"

"There are no gypsies here, but there once was one."

"I figured as much."

"It's named for a fortune teller that came through these parts years ago, back in the Depression days, during the Prohibition."

"That's a while ago, my friend."

"Longer than I've been around, but my Grandma Pickering knew of her. She said the woman was the real deal. 'Fortunes lost and found, read and told, by the all-knowing, all-seeing, Madam Luna' – that's what Grandma Pickering said was on the side of her caravan."

"Caravan? I wouldn't have thought the circus came through these parts," I said.

"No, they never have mister, but she wasn't with any circus. They said she was traveling up and down the coast on her own, telling people what they needed to hear, not what they wanted to hear – if you know what I mean. Grandma Pickering said that's what made her special, or different."

"She must have been if they named a bridge after her."

"Nope!" he smiled. "Its real name is Josiah Huxley Bridge, for the old Civil War hero. We just call it Gypsy's Bluff because of what happened there so long ago. And what's there now – haunted as it is by the Lady in Gray – the Gangster's Doll."

"Creepy haunted, huh," I said, "Like Casper?"

"Casper was a friendly ghost," he replied. "This one's not too happy. She'll mess with your head as much as scare the shit out of you."

"Ha, ha," I laughed. "That's why your friend Harvey wouldn't give me directions?"

"That, and because he's a pain in the ass."

"Okay then, why are you telling me this?"

"Because I can see it in your eyes like I've seen it in the eyes of hundreds of others over the years – you're gonna spend the next three hours trying to find that bridge to save yourself an hour's drive. The fact is it's only a few miles up the road. But there are no signs and if you're an outta-towner you'll most likely get lost. And someone will have to go and find you. And because I work for the town, and tonight I'm on call, that person will be me. So, if you get in your Jeep and follow me, I'll show you the way and tell you the full story when we get there, and then you can stay there as long as you want, or go to wherever it is you're going."

"Fair enough," I said. "I'm game, and thanks. My name's Crosby," I added, and reached out and shook his hand.

The pump stopped abruptly at twenty dollars. I tapped out what gas was left in the nozzle and hung it back onto the pump. Dean took off in his pickup, and dammit, I got in my car and followed him. Don't ask me why I agreed to follow a complete stranger who could have been pulling my leg as easily as the cord on his bloodstained chainsaw, down a country road in the middle of nowhere to save myself a little time and gas. But I did. Somehow, I thought there would be a good story in it. Maybe he really would tell me a secret.

He was driving at a good clip, too – he knew the roads. At the fork where Harvey told me to bang a 'Luther,' we hung a 'Roger.' From there on, the road narrowed considerably. The pavement was broken, bumpy, crumbled and patched. The forest stood at the road's edge. Great trees leaned in over us. Their long and thick, twisted limbs formed a natural canopy over the road. It was like driving through a tunnel. In the headlights the branches cast long shadows that looked like gnarled fingers of ancient hags reaching for the hearts and souls of the Brothers Grimm.

If all the roads around here were like this, I began to realize why Mondays were so busy for Dean. I've driven up north, deep into the Woods of Maine, up in the wilderness of Piscataquis County that Harvey mentioned. Moose there outnumber humanity. They will walk, run, lope, and stride right out in front of you like they own the road. I know because I nearly clipped a cow and her calf one early evening a summer ago. Now I felt like it could happen here any second. The trees were simply too close to the road for one of those beasts to even bother to hesitate and stop.

Dean accelerated around a curve and so did I. My old Jeep four-door was clinging for its life as I managed the curve and every damn pothole the road had to offer. He slowed and took a right, drove a quarter mile and took a left. Went about another half mile and I followed him around a sharp bend to the right. I had just straightened my wheels when Dean's brake lights flashed. I thought for sure something had jumped out in front of him – a deer or even a moose. But no. The road had widened slightly and he pulled over to his right, to the side of the road, and stopped. Just before he shut off his lights I caught the glare of reflectors ahead, on either side of the road. We were already at the bridge. That prick Harvey was actually going to send me an hour out of my way?

Dean jumped out of his pickup truck and reached into the bed in one motion. Fast enough that visions of an insane McCulloch-wielding maniac flashed through my head. But he pulled out a can of beer instead, cracked the lid, took a sip, then stretched and yawned.

"This is it," he yelled out. "You want a beer?"

"Why not," I yelled back from my Jeep. If there was an echo, it was swallowed by the forest. I turned off my headlights and Dean disappeared. The pale green glow of the dashboard blinded me until I shut off the engine. When I got out I could smell the brine in the air, but I damn well couldn't see where it was coming from, let alone a bridge or anything else. Darkness was complete. The forest was pitch – on the other side of black. I couldn't even see the stars above because of the canopy from the trees. But I could easily see why anyone would creep out here. But driving through? Other than that bear of a road – probably wouldn't notice a thing.

"Here you go," he said.

"Thanks." I could hear him before I could see him. I reached out like a blind man for his hand until I touched a cold beer. "I tell you, a black bear could walk in front of me right now and I wouldn't see it until he took a chunk out of me."

"Your eyes will adjust to the dark in a few minutes," he said. "There's no black bears in Maine ever eaten anyone – other than that poor bastard up north just a year ago this last June."

"What!"

"Just a fluke, they said – wrong place at the wrong time."

"I just – I hadn't heard – that's all."

"Once they found him they clamped the story shut real quick – right at the beginning of summer tourist season it was."

"What a way to go."

"The news isn't quick to report such things, Crosby – not at the beginning of tourist season. It tends to piss people off."

"Piss people off?"

"Yessah. There was a murderer on the loose up there a few summers back. The bastard killed his girlfriend because she didn't want to be his girlfriend. Happened late May or early June, I think – just before the summer tourist season. He disappeared into the woods and they couldn't find him. 'A killer on the run in the Woods of Maine' – it was headline news for months. Forget about anyone going up north to Vacationland that summer – a lot of people were scared off. Businesses – mom and pop, big and small, they lost their arse. Summertime is when a lot of them make their nut. Finally, they stopped advertising. Then the media stopped blathering and they learned their lesson. The line between public information and private profit is very fine. You can only sell so many papers but you can never sell enough advertising. So, Crosby, I'm not surprised you didn't hear about the man-eating black bear. They swallowed that story quicker than the bear swallowed that poor fella."

"That's fairly gruesome imagery, Dean," I said. "You don't have to convince me."

"Consider it a reminder – the wilderness can be a cruel mistress."

"I'm beginning to wonder." And I really was.

"There's plenty of time for that – the night is young."

"What about that murderer? When did they catch him?"

"They didn't," he answered plain as day.

"Holy shit!"

"Ha! Calm down – he turned himself in. Walked right through town – the length of Main Street – to the sheriff's office or police station – I can't remember which – and turned himself in. Give or take three or four months in the woods. He survived black fly season, but was worried he wouldn't make it through hunting season without a bullet in his back – the friggin' coward."

"You're inspiring me, Dean, but maybe this isn't such a good idea after all. I'm not sure what the point of all of this is – of why you're telling me this instead of about the Gangster's Doll, that Lady in Gray."

"That's simple – you commented about a black bear taking a chunk out of you and I reassured you through example how unlikely that could happen." He paused for a gulp of beer. "But I also wanted to impress upon you that murder can and does and has happened in rural Maine. That's what happened to poor Lillian Saunders – the Gangster's

Doll. She was murdered right here." He cast a shadowy gesture in the direction of the bridge. "In 1932. She'd been gone a little over a week when a passing fisherman spotted her from his dory. She was face down with a bullet in her back, a few paces from the road but down the embankment. You have to understand, back then this place was not as busy as it is nowadays." He paused, maybe for a sip of beer, or maybe, considering the lack of traffic, to let the irony soak in. Either-or, I imagined he was smiling at those words, except that I couldn't see the can of beer I was putting to my lips let alone his face.

"The find was unsightly, *gruesome* as you can imagine," he continued. "They were only certain it was her because she'd lost the top part of her ring finger on her left hand while working in a fish cannery when she was a teenager."

"Whoa," I breathed. "You know, for a guy who just collects road kill you sure know a lot about what's going on around here."

"Haha!" he laughed. "That SOB Harvey – he can be such a ball buster."

I nodded, and said, "Yup, he sure can."

"He is right, that's part of the job, collecting road kill. I'm head of the public works department. It *is* my job to know a lot about what's going on around here. But the only reason I know so much about Lillian Saunders is because she was best friends with my Grandma Pickering."

"Now I understand."

"Nobody else did. Why Lillian would even associate with that gangster. It's a very sad story and, I know, it's not the first time it's ever been told. Grandma said it was because he flashed a lot of money when he was in town. He had a big Packard, a fine suit, and a wad of cash. The Depression was full on and she fell for it – him, the money – whatever he was offering.

"My grandma knew that Lillian had seen the gypsy fortune teller. Lillian had told her so. The gypsy warned her to stay far from that man for she was placing herself in the presence of evil. But Lillian thought it was a bluff – that her friends had put the gypsy up to it – to end the affair."

"So, she called the gypsy's bluff," I said, "And lost the bet."

"She sure did, Crosby," he said. "Really wasn't sure what happened – what set him off enough to kill her – officially anyway. When the gypsy woman came through town the following autumn my grandma went to see her, asked if she could offer any insight into Lillian's fate, and she did. Madam Luna said Lillian had told the gangster playfully that she knew all about him – too much for a murderous bastard to hear – that a fortune teller had warned her about him. He then sweet talked her into driving away with him. You see, it wasn't like she went missing, she left town on her own. Told her mama she'd got a job down in Portland. That's why nobody looked for her. Instead, the numb girl got into the big Packard early one evening and was never seen alive again. Because she was shot in the back they figured she was running away from him, but Madam Luna said otherwise. Somehow he lured her from the car. She stepped from the Packard – to look for something or at something – something he had for her, Madam Luna said. What exactly – who knows?" He shrugged his shoulders and sighed. "She's still looking for that something, they say, whatever it was she was looking for that night she stepped from the car, her spirit still wanders the bridge looking for what she lost, and she'll continue to haunt the bridge until she finds it."

"What's your guess?"

"What she's looking for?"

I nodded.

"It's something precious to her, grandma said, or she wouldn't keep looking. Such futility – to seek that which was lost, to lose something so dear, to have it within your grasp one moment and have it slip away the next – forever. There's only one thing it could be."

"What's that?"

"I believe it's what Grandma Pickering always said it was – her innocence."

I took another hit of beer and so did Dean. My eyes had adjusted to the darkness now. There was a moon out there somewhere, rising. I could see out onto the bridge, and see the winding road that was carved out of the steep embankment on the opposite side.

"She's been seen countless times over the years, and when she does show herself it's when folks least expect it. Kayakers going under the bridge have looked up and seen her there above them. Fishermen have

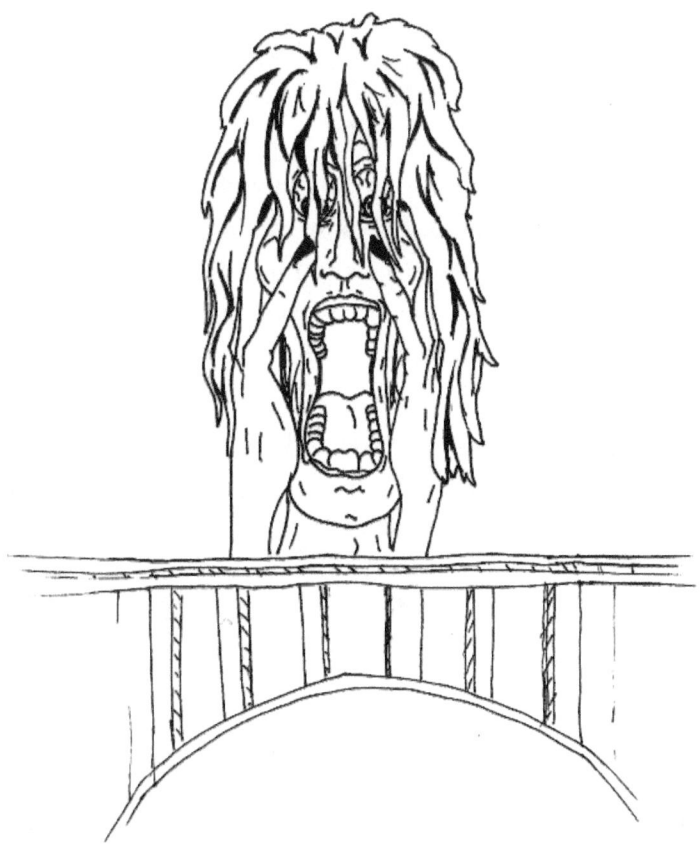

seen her walking along the bridge from the shoreline. Couples come here to park and see a left handprint – with part of the ring finger missing – suddenly form out of the condensation on the car window. People driving over the bridge have glanced in their rear-view mirror and seen her in their backseats – and drove their cars into the railing. Unsuspecting people have actually pulled over and offered her a lift – and she's ridden into town with them – only to vanish somewhere along the way. Stuff like that. Two weeks ago a couple was coming back from dinner over on Moose Harbor. They turned onto the bridge and, as they did, a women suddenly appeared seemingly from nowhere. She was standing in the middle of the road and he drove right into her. Except when he got out of his car there was no one there – nothing – no sign of anyone – no damage to the car. His wife was on the phone, frantic as hell, calling 911 when he told her to hang up. It just goes on and on."

"That sounds crazy."

"Yes it does, and I keep telling myself that. You know why, Crosby?" I gave him a shrug. "Because that couple that hit the woman in the middle of the road was me and my wife. What happened is still fresh in my head. I can't shake it. Everyone thinks it's a game until they see her and see how real *it* really is. Things are never the same for you after that. You go to church, listen to all the big talk about life and death and the hereafter. Let me assure you, it doesn't have the same edge once you've partaken from the forbidden cup, get a taste of what's on the other side. So let me ask you something. Are you certain this is what you want to do?"

"Me? I'm just trying to make my way to Moose Harbor."

"Ha, ha!" he laughed. "After this beer I'm gonna leave, and you're gonna be here by yourself at this haunted bridge. All alone. Something may or may not happen. If it does, are you sure that you're ready to live with it?"

I thought about that for more than a few seconds – the imagery of the Gangster's Doll walking up behind me and asking for a light or something, or worse, confusing me with the bastard who did her in. All of a sudden, I was having second thoughts about how I'd approached this whole expedition, and wondering if it was a bad idea.

"I haven't been entirely upfront with you, Dean," I said. "I think it's time I laid my cards on the table."

"What are you saying?" he asked with a serious tone.

"I actually came here to specifically find out what I could about the Gangster's Doll."

"Damn you," he snapped at me. His anger took me by surprise. I stepped back, but then he burst out laughing. "No shite, Sherlock!"

"You knew? But how?"

"Could it be more obvious? I gave you a good look at the chainsaw. Anyone else would have surely gone the opposite direction real fast if a complete stranger with a blood splattered chainsaw asked them to follow him into the woods."

"Now that you mention it," I said.

"This isn't my first dance, you know. I figure you're either a nutter or a ghost hunter."

"I'm a writer, actually," I chuckled, "A bit of a nutter, too, I suppose, and a pretty lousy poker player."

"I hope you don't write as bad as you play poker," he smiled.

"Oh, I'm good at what I do. My boss sent me up here, wanted a ghost story for the October issue – firsthand account. I wasn't sure what it was or is I'm looking for – about the Gangster's Doll – so instead of being direct, I thought I'd act dumb."

"Well, I assure you, you're a pretty good actor."

At that we both laughed. I couldn't disagree and was about to say as much to my new-found friend when out of the dark from across the bridge headlights appeared from an oncoming car. It was moving at a good clip, too, winding its way along the road, right up until it approached the bridge and slowed. It came to a full stop, but then, after a few seconds continued over the bridge. The big Plymouth pulled up next to us. There were two in the front and two in back. The guy behind the wheel rolled down his window. He looked like he was twenty-ish going on fifteen. "Hey – you guys seen the Lady in Gray – the Gangster's Doll?" he asked. "Or is this all a gypsy's bluff?" The remark was followed by nervous giggles from within the car.

"We just got here ourselves," I said.

"No action yet," said Dean, "But she'll be by to visit soon enough."

"Seriously man?" the driver asked.

Dean nodded. "She'll show up when you least expect it. She always does. You gotta be patient."

"Mind if we join you?"

"I don't, and I don't think she'll mind either," Dean said. "After all, she's still looking for her man, and it just might be you." He pointed at the driver.

"Damn!" The guy swallowed hard. He pulled the Plymouth to the side of the road.

They all got out quickly. It was difficult to see their faces in the darkness. I could just make out their forms, a couple of dudes and their dates. They were young enough, and right away they began to yammer like we weren't even there.

"I can't believe we're doing this," said the taller gal.

"You best believe we're doing it, Tara," said the driver.

"Yeah, well, I don't know if I am ready to see a ghost, Blake." Tara sounded unsure. "Maybe this isn't the best idea."

"You wanted to be a part of a ghost story. Now you are," Blake replied to her.

"That's a line from a movie," said the other guy.

"No it's not, Ricky," Blake said.

"For real, dude," he answered.

"I don't care if it is or not, you two," said Tara. "I'm really starting to feel spooked."

"I'm pretty sure you have nothing to worry about," Ricky said.

"You say that about everything, Ricky," said Blake.

"I liked the story, but I don't know how much of it – if any – is real," Ricky answered. "I don't know how much of it is true. I think the bartender just wanted to go home so he told us a tall tale to send us on our merry way."

"No way!" Tara shouted. "My folks have been talking about the Gangster's Doll for as long as we've been coming up here, and that's like – forever!"

Dean exhaled wearily.

"Hey mister," said Blake. "It's true, right?"

They were annoying as hell and were crushing my vibe in a big way. Somehow, all the experience of being here in the moment was lost on them – or maybe it was lost on me. With all their chattering I didn't know what was going to come of this excursion into the unknown. It seemed like they had ruined any chance of anything happening.

But I was happy I'd met Dean. He was a good egg, as they say. Truth was, at the very least, with all that he had already shared with me, I figured I had enough for a good story now anyway. Fact is, people don't want actual proof that there is such a thing as ghosts, a ghostly realm or some kind of cosmic afterlife. They wouldn't trust their own lying eyes if a ghost passed right in front of them. Nope. The only thing people want is something stimulating and sexy to chew on but not swallow. That way they can sleep peacefully at night – happily exist believing in God without believing that He is one such ghost in such a cosmic afterlife.

"Your friend, she really doesn't talk that much does she," said Dean. "I think I like her."

"Tara?" asked Blake. "She could talk the ears off a deaf priest hearing confession."

"Pah-leeze, Blake," she responded.

"No, the other one with you," Dean replied. He glanced around. "Wait … where …?" He stopped short.

"What other girl?" Ricky asked. "You mean *your* friend?" He looked behind us.

"Where is she?" said Tara. "She was just by the Jeep."

"No," I said. "I saw four of you get out of that Plymouth." I pointed to the car.

"What!" Blake shouted. "Stop it! Stop messing with us, man!"

"That woman was already here," said Ricky. "She was standing with you when we got here."

"And I saw another gal climb out of the back seat when you parked," Dean said firmly.

"She stepped out right behind you, Tara," I added.

"Oh, no! No! No!" Tara panicked. "I really think it's time we left, Blake," she pleaded.

"La-listen man," Ricky stammered. "This isn't cool."

"Seriously guys," said Blake, and he pointed at my Jeep. "She *was* ... there ... look."

I followed his hand. We all did. To a patch of condensation that seemed to glow, ever so pale, on the driver's side of my windshield, as though someone sitting behind the wheel had just breathed on it. That was all fine and good – but for the slender, feminine, four-and-a-half fingered handprint that formed in the middle of it, a lefty at that, impressed upon the glass right in front our lying eyes.

*An innocent boy, mesmerized by a midway at a county fair,
chances upon a curious attraction and soon discovers
what memories are really made of.*

The Barker and the Pinwheel and That Game of Karma

"Step right up," the barker shouted out at the gathering swarm of rubes in front of his booth. "You there – in the red plaid shirt and the shit-eating grin. Come here and try your luck."

"Me?" I asked innocently, and jerked my thumb at my chest. I was standing there by myself gawking and smiling, true, but very much unaware that the said smile on my face was in any way indicating a desire on my part to dive into a bowlful of shit. But what did I know? My head was still ringing. That being because minutes before I had walked into a light post while staring at the freak-show preview. I was with my cousin Scooter when the freaks came out and paraded across a small stage in front of the show's tent. A few odd looking folk – a woman in a bathing suit as hairy as an ape, a wolf-faced man yipping and howling, and a square-headed hunchback who waved a hand with six fingers. On the stage, a big man in a bowler hat challenged a small, but growing crowd of onlookers, "To enter if you dare! View humanity's damned and damn strange at the sake of your own sanity and peril." I might have entered, but for that lamp post, how it just walked right up and slammed me. It left me feeling fuzzy headed, like I had wandered in from a dream.

Music from a barrel organ had lured me away from the freaks and further down the midway. There, I had spied the barker out of the crowd. He stood before his booth of wood and canvas, brightly lit with globe string lights and, oddly, adorned with stuffed animal heads – bear, elk, deer, and wolf. I couldn't tell if they were real or the toy prizes. There was an elaborate back mural, too – a painting of an exotic forest and mountain range with a lonely, rustic cabin tucked away in a corner. I watched him for a minute or two as he joked and ribbed each and every rube passerby on the midway. A master carny, I thought. There was a personality about him for sure. He was bulky and tall, or seemed tall. Maybe because of the oversized top hat he had squeezed onto his melon-sized head. Damn big head. You couldn't miss it. His face was round, too, and so were his eyeballs. They were more like a set of pinballs rolling around his sockets. Such an impressive set of peepers, but nothing compared to the size of his schnoz. It was though a goose had lost an egg, or maybe planted it there. Truth be told – a confession: it was that beak of his that made me smile wide – a grin wide enough to suppose on his part that my appetite was whetted for a steaming bowl of shit, as mentioned.

"Yeah, I was talking to you kid," he continued, as though to dismiss any doubts I had. "I've been watching you watching me for a while."

"You have?" I said surprised.

"Oh, yeah," he grinned. "You're curious to play my game, aren't yah?"

"I guess so."

"You guess?" he feigned dismay. "There's nothing to guess here. You gotta be a special person. You gotta know what you're looking for – if you want to win the game. You do wanna win the game, don't yah?"

I nodded my head eagerly.

"What are you looking for?"

"A way back," I replied.

"Oh, really," he said. "From where?"

"Why, from where I came, mister," I answered him, like it was a matter of fact.

"You really want to find your way back, then?"

I nodded once more.

"Well then, I think it's time." He rubbed his hands together in anticipation. "You wanna try your luck at Karma?"

That raised my eyebrows. It was the first time I had ever heard the word and I almost blurted out, "What's that?", which would have only further confirmed my status as a taste-bud challenged rube from the Woods of Maine.

"Well, kid, you wanna play the game or not?" he asked me again. "Try it for *free* – the first game's on *me*."

I was lost in thought and still gawking at his nose. The people around me were not staring at his nose, but at me – waiting on my answer. I wondered if I should. Grandpa and Uncle Denny had let me and Scooter loose on the fairgrounds so they could go off and watch the ox pull in peace. That was an hour ago. I had since lost my cousin Scooter to the freak show. Enchanted he was by the bushy wiles of the hairy woman. I really was thinking I should go back and look for him, but instead, for a reason I'll never know or understand, I asked, "How do you play?"

That set the pinballs spinning and bouncing in their sockets. He reached up and pulled the big hat from his head. Placed it gently over his heart and leaned forward, like he was going to share the secrets of the Vatican with me, and me alone. His breath reeked of herring, or maybe sardines. I knew the smell very well. I had an aunt named Trudy who had a similar air about her, in the way an air seems to waft from every crack, crevice, and orifice of old people like sour milk and day-old steamed broccoli. Aunt Trudy would take dried herring or a can of sardines and crackers with her tea each afternoon. For some reason, she was always frustrated by my reluctance to join her for tea. Her breath and body smelled like the gill nets of a Nova Scotia trawler. Years later, when I dated an amateur whore named Victoria, I would be confronted by a similar odor from time to time in her presence. In my naiveté at first, I assumed she too had an affinity for sardines and crackers, which I found odd. It always confounded me until an acquaintance of mine by the name of Johnson visually informed me of her amateur status one evening at a social. He enlightened me in the most subtle of ways, standing there in the back parlor with his Johnson rod stuck in her gaping maw, accompanied by a shrug and two thumbs up. In retrospect, it may have seemed like a mighty blow – for me and him – I suppose. But the worst of it was later that night, when the girl and I broke it off. She kissed me goodbye before I could react, and walked out the door. Talk about your awkward moments – by any standard. The days and weeks that followed were gut-wrenching. The aftermath left me alone with the demons of rage and despair that accompany willful abandonment and betrayal – that and the most fretful of quandaries – by allowing her kiss goodbye upon my innocent lips, did it make me gay by proxy?

But that was in another life, somewhere later in time. In this one, at the carnival, I could not have imagined such things, not then as a young teenager, with the barker leaning forward in my face as though to impart a truth unknown to me yet in my small but ever expanding universe. I stared into the cavernous hollow of his nostrils. If I told you he was close enough for me to count each and every hair in that snot drop, you'd probably think I was exaggerating. Perhaps, for the interior of that honker was as thick and lush as the flora of a tropical rain forest. The reality was, there were so many hairs I wasn't even sure I could count that high.

"Karma's not a game, kid," he shouted out. I jumped and inhaled a gust of dead fish funk in the process. "Karma's the force of life. It's up. It's down. It's what's good and what's bad. Sometimes, one leads to another – the highs and lows. It comes and goes. It's filled with positive and negative charged particles – positively!" A wide grin stretched across his face. His eyeballs bulged. "Karma spins around and round like a wheel – like, say, a wheel like this!" Like a magician on stage, like a rabbit out of a hat, he pulled a pinwheel from the depths of his topper. It was balanced on a long-stemmed, ornately carved wand, maybe a foot or more in length. He held the base carefully, gently between his forefinger and thumb. It drew my attention momentarily from the wheel, because I noticed the shape of the stem resembled the leg of some kind of canine. A wolf's perhaps. But the base of the wand gave me second thoughts about what kind of animal it was formerly attached to. It was an oversized paw of a beast of some kind. Its claws were extended, the nails curved like scimitars, sharp as a razor's edge, ready to strike out at its prey. I touched my throat and swallowed hard, imagining what one swipe from that thing could do to me.

"Ha! Don't worry kid," he said, seeming to read my mind. "The pure of heart have nothing to fear. The paw's a reminder to those others who ponder such things as darkness – of the world that is or the world that could be if they play with karma." He then waved the wand lazily in front of my face. The thing began to bend like rubber and the pinwheel turned slowly. "When you play the game of Karma, one simple trigger word or phrase can make or break the pure of heart." My hand dropped from my throat to my sides as I fixed on the pinwheel and wand. "Maybe you want to test your skills? Have a chance to show one and all what you're really made of?"

I did not reply, but my head bobbed hypnotically like a Manchurian candidate's.

"Play the game?" He continued to wave the wand, and the pinwheel moved steadily.

"Play?" I mumbled. Hell, I was already in the game.

"Let's see what your karma is then, kid, shall we? Be ready – your fate is mine and it's about to unfold before you." He paused for a moment, then added, "Remember, never turn your back on monsters in a hallucination."

I could hear laughter around me. An ox bellowed in the distance. I thought of my uncle and grandfather standing ankle deep in all kinds of bullshit. That damn barrel organ played sporadically somewhere on the midway. I wondered if Scooter had found true love at the freak show.

And then I heard the barker's words echo in my head, "…your fate is mine" and "never turn your back on monsters!"

"Wait! No!" I tried to shout out to no avail. The pinwheel had rendered me speechless. My thoughts went adrift. Background chatter and static filled the void. The pinwheel gained speed, spinning counterclockwise – gliding in a spiral like a Catherine wheel out of control. But to me, as I stared at the thing, focused on the center, I began to conceptualize the center of the center of all things. In my mind's eye, I found that center – and went into an inner-stellar overdrive. As the barker continued to wave the wand, the wheel spun a magic web. It seemed to expand in size. It began to take form. Something like the flow of the milky galaxies in the night sky above, clear and clean of all the light pollution city folk must endure and emit, which, in the greatest of ironies, blinds them from the light above. That which I speak of and what we know of as the heavens.

And thusly, the pinwheel took the form of a mighty galaxy before my eyes, spinning and shooting stars across the wheel like the Perseid Meteor Shower across the universe. The more he waved the wand, the faster the pinwheel spiraled, the greater the center expanded, and the more I became drawn to it. Years later, in another life, somewhere in time, when I accidentally took a hit of purple haze instead of the acetaminophen pain reliever I thought I was taking for a headache, I would achieve the same degree of clarity then, when the lysergic acid diethylamide saturated the gray matter between my ears, as I did that moment when I was mesmerized by the pinwheel. Total consciousness. Awareness. One with being. The Universal Father. Conceptual totality. It was liberating and thought provoking. In a magic carpet ride sort of way. There was no past or future – only a present presence – the here, now, and all that was and would be.

This was no ordinary barker.

That's what I was thinking when I opened my eyes. I was flat out on my back deep in a forest somewhere. It was an ancient, old growth forest, I was sure of that. The trees shot up to the heavens. The tops could have daubed the starry palette of the night sky above they were so high. I wondered if I was, actually. More so, I wondered how I even got here – wherever here was.

In the near distance I could hear howling – coyotes or wolves, I could only guess. For all I knew I could have been in Siberia or snuggled under Parson's Drop on the backside of Mount Agamenticus. I was kind of hoping for the latter. Even though the woods there are said to be haunted by a witch, at least they were closer to my home on Moose Harbor. That also meant that the sound of wild canines howling would be coyotes, not wolves.

"Not meant to be," I heard a voice whisper nearby. I raised my head quickly and looked in every direction.

"Who said that?" I called out. A shadow passed from tree to tree off to my right.

"I can hear you loud enough," the voice whispered. "Pity you found your way here."

"I'm not afraid," I lied.

"You should be," the voice laughed. "He's coming."

At that, I heard a thrashing in the forest. Moments passed as it grew louder, closer. Suddenly, a man stumbled into the clearing where I waited. I had sat up by then and he was looking down on me panting heavily and gasping for air.

"Help me!" he begged. Before I could respond, he repeated it in Spanish, I'm sure, and German, I think. I had seen enough World War II movies that I knew the ring of German when I heard it. The greater mystery was why he was speaking either language at all. No. Check that – why did he need help at all? What was he running from? And then the howls erupted again, and this time they were not very far off. "For the love of God, do you understand me?" he shouted.

"Yes," I answered and jumped to my feet. "What the hell is that howling?"

"Are you insane?" he pleaded, "or are you one of them?" His face turned to realization. "Holy God! You are one!" He stepped toward me with madness in his eyes.

"Whoa!" I held up my hand in defense and said the first thing that came into my head. "I am traveling through the countryside."

"In this land?" he asked incredulously. "On your way to the torture palace? Maybe? To Colonia Dignidad? Yes!"

"To what?" I replied, utterly confused. He stepped closer to me, wiped his grubby, damp, dirty hands across his chest. Smiled a vicious smile of death calling. "Who ... are ... you?" I asked.

"Reverend Paolo," he whispered in my ear, "of the Church of the Once Redeemed." He leaned back, as though to relax, but then lunged, and grabbed me by the collar. Pulled me close to his face. His eyes bore into mine. He breathed deeply. His breath was foul and his teeth decayed. "Tell me? Who were you? What did you do? Before the war?"

I shook my head slowly. "What war?" I answered.

"Yes," he nodded. "I had almost forgotten. It's so easy to forget. They make you forget. I am a prisoner, too."

The howling erupted again, which, in that moment, I reasoned, saved me from his deranged clutches, for he released me.

"What the hell are those things?" I demanded.

He looked at me with curiosity. A moment of clarity or trust, I did not know, but he whispered frantically, "Andean Wolves – the monsters of Patagonia, you fool! They have been unleashed by their masters at the Colony. I escaped to tell the world. But now we're being hunted."

Instantly my mind went to the barker and his wand. I pictured the claw at its base and imagined the creature attached to it. I shuddered in holy terror. I could not imagine a beast that savage in the wild let alone coming face-to-face with it. I could hear the barker's cackling laugh inside my head.

"Follow me," I snapped, and began to run wildly in the opposite direction from the howling. The path was narrow, but I stayed on it, ducking under low boughs of pines, running through broad-leafed plants, and leaping over fallen trees. The ground was level and soft. Ahead of me, I noticed a dim light through the forest. The path was leading us right toward it. "Almost there," I puffed. The path widened, and the light grew brighter.

"Hurry," he squealed. "They're getting closer."

They were. I could hear the brush behind us thrash and snap.

"We're just about there," I breathed. Where that was I did not know. I had no idea. With a little luck we could be making a mad dash into the Alamo. But ... suddenly, I was struck by the fear. The Colony he mentioned – the torture palace. What if we were being herded instead of hunted? I heard the first growl, then the savage snapping of jaws. Holy be-Jesus! Where had that barker landed me? If this was karma I did not want any part of it.

"There," he shouted. It was a cabin.

"I see it!" I said. The path emptied into a backyard, more a clearing. I didn't care. Growls, ferocious and foreboding, closed in all around. They were just about on us.

"Help!" Paolo shouted. "Let us in!"

I made for the back porch and jumped the three steps – rushed the door with all I had, expecting it to be bolted.

"Please open the door," I heard his desperate plea behind me. "There's no ... ahhhhh-yeeee!"

The scream was horrific.

I hear it now.

Bloodcurdling.

In my head it resides.

The echo.

Awakens in those lonely moments when all is silent.

When all else has passed into the night.

Amidst the fury of the savage mauling behind me his screams ceased abruptly. I slammed into the cabin door with all my strength and, as I did so, turned to face my maker. But the door gave way. I fell backward and landed hard on my ass. I bolted upright and looked back out on the yard but could see nothing in the darkness. All had quieted. In desperation I kicked the door shut with my foot. I reached up, bolted it tight and waited for the onslaught of beasts to slam into it. My heart pounded in anticipation. Adrenaline pumped through me. Cold sweat bubbled up and seeped out profusely. I tried to catch my breath, felt the hyperventilation overcome me and I near puked.

I fell back. Shut my eyes and wondered at the horror.

Why?

What has happened to me?

Was this karma?

"Not your typical game," I heard a voice whisper nearby.

I opened my eyes abruptly. "Who said that?"

"The wheel spins, and so does life."

"What the ..." My eyes adjusted. I found myself in a dimly lit, high-ceilinged room – clean, cozy, rustic. A wide, central chimney rose through the cabin. Below it, a fire blazed brightly under the mantel of a large stone hearth. Two armchairs were positioned in front of the hearth. But for a small table between them, the arms would have touched. On the table a cup of tea steamed next to an open magazine of crossword puzzles. To my left, through a window slightly ajar, an owl hooted. There, from that side of the room, heads and shoulders of large animals projected out from the wall as though they were bursting through it and about to stampede into the room – moose and deer and elk and bison. So curious to me – I could see a hint of suffering in their listless, glass eyes. I turned away, imagining what had just happened outside, attempting to shake the thoughts from my head. To the right of the fireplace was an archway to another room – lit. From it, a matronly woman entered the room – kind, dark eyes, silver hair, a loving smile. She wore a flower print dress and slippers. In her hand she held a tray with cookies.

"Why, Jonathan," she said. "What in heavens are you doing on the floor?"

"Aunt Trudy?" I asked more than said. It was her, but an even older version of her.

"Yes, Jonathan?" she answered, and placed the tray down on the small table near the tea.

I didn't know what to say. Hell, I didn't even know where I was. Maybe that was just it. Was I in a room or was I in a room in someone's head? "The ... the wolves, the man out ... outside," I stammered and pointed toward the door.

"Oh, dear," said my aunt in a concerned tone. "Not the barker's pinwheel again? That game of Karma?"

"Huh?" I said.

"You must have had another episode."

"I was just at the fair with grandpa and Uncle Denny," I said before all she said sunk in.

She looked at me with sadness.

"Wait! Another episode?" I asked. "What episode?"

"That was 25 years ago, Jonathan. Before the war."

"Before the war?"

"You poor boy," she said with a tsk-tsk.

That's when I noticed myself – the first time since the woods – I was not a boy! I looked at my hands, their size. I touched my face and felt stubble on my chin. I saw the length of my legs and the size of my feet. I stood up and was a half-foot taller than Aunt Trudy. "What in God's name has happened to me, auntie?" I noticed a bathroom and stepped toward its door.

"You don't want to do that just yet," my aunt said.

I did not listen, but rushed past her into the bathroom.

"Please, don't do it to yourself Jonathan!" she pleaded with me. "Don't!"

I stood before the mirror over the sink. The waves pulsed through me, shock and disbelief. My heart raced. I did not know the man in the mirror. "Who am I?" I saw the man's lips move and heard my voice, but it was not me. I stared blankly for minutes, touching my nose, my ears, the sides of my face. I gasped. A tear welled up in my eye and trailed down my cheek. "I was at the fair," I said above a whisper. "It was my turn at the wheel – the man called me up. The barker. He spun it and it went around and around. I could see the stars and Milky Way," I trailed off in despair. This couldn't really have happened. "It was as though I ..."

"... was on a magic carpet ride," she interrupted. She took my hand in hers and led me to the armchairs before the fire. "Sit, my dear, please." She was comforting, as I had always found her to be ... or to have been ... or – God, please no – to still be at this moment. I sat, and she did, too. If all of this was anywhere near real, I had lost my childhood – my life – somewhere in time.

"What happened," I asked her.

"We're really not sure what happened to you, child," she answered me. "They said some type of hypnotic regression occurred. It's as though you got stuck in time on that day at the fair." She paused and picked up the cup of tea. The steam was gone now, but she still blew gently before she sipped. I could not take my eyes off the tea. Smiling, she placed the cup down and said, "Let me fetch you a cup, Jonathan."

I shook my head and said, "No thank you."

"Don't be silly, I can tell you want a cup – now," and she went into the kitchen.

"Now?" I thought.

In a moment she returned. "There," Aunt Trudy said, placing it down next to the tray. "It's out of a fresh kettle. Do be careful. It's very hot."

I picked it up, blew on the tea. It had a funky aroma, but I took a couple of sips anyway. "Foo – bitter," I said. I would have spit it out but for my aunt in the line of fire.

"Well, it's plain – no sugar or milk. Just the way you like it."

"Weird aftertaste," I said.

"You don't have to drink anymore," she said, and took the cup from me. We stared into the fire. The flames and embers snapped and popped. "It's not as bad as it used to be – in fact you haven't had a lapse like this in a few years. We always know when you've slipped back in time – to that day at the fair I mean – because of the man and the wolves chasing you right here to the door." She looked over at it. "Yup. Bolted again." She gave a sigh. "You always manage to find your way here, though, to the cabin where you were raised."

The impossibility of the moment overwhelmed me. I buried my head in the palms of my hands. I had never known loneliness or imagined what it must feel like. I was pretty sure this was it – hopeless and helpless. The sensation gnawed at my insides. I thought, "How could I have lost twenty-five years of my life? What was twenty-five years of life like? I was only a fourteen-year-old kid. Hell, I am a fourteen-year-old kid."

I thought of the barker – his big schnoz – and I attempted a halfhearted smile. I thought of the game – Karma – the pinwheel spinning – the universe opening up before me. Then I remembered what she had just said – the cabin where you were raised? I wasn't raised in a cabin.

"Aunt Trudy!" I lifted my head. She had left the room. The fire had died down, too, which filled the room with long shadows that flickered across the walls. How much time had passed? Had I fallen asleep? I stood, felt a little lightheaded. "Aunt Trudy?" I called her name once more, but there was no reply. Outside, the owl hooted again. I looked over at the window, which was no longer ajar but wide open. A gust shot through it, lifting the drapes. When it struck me goosebumps rippled up and down my arm. My hair stood on edge. Not because of the gust, but because of the low growl I heard near the window. Suddenly something on the wall moved. The shadows shifted and it wasn't because of the fire. I panicked and did what anyone else in that situation would do. I grabbed a lantern near the door and stepped toward the window. The light wasn't much, but I could see the wall well enough to know the game of Karma was spinning wildly out of control. The deer and elk and other animals were gone. Replaced by the heads and shoulders of different animals – bizarre or extinct creatures – a gigantic reptilian thing and a saber-toothed tiger, a komodo dragon and a dire wolf, and a massive bear – all mounted in macabre displays, the agony of death and rage still frozen in a paralytic grip upon their faces. If all of this was a nightmarish hallucination at the hands of that scheming barker, now would be the time when one of those things would lunge at me. My heart would split open. I'd shit my pants. On the other hand, considering that the moose and buffalo, etc., had now become savage, primordial beasts readying to devour me, maybe this was a hallucination within a hallucination. Yet, on the other hand, I didn't even know where the hell I was. But was this real? I pinched myself – slapped my face silly – that hurt. I stared at the monsters on the wall long enough to wonder if they were staring back at me. I stepped back slowly as I feebly attempted to convince myself I was imagining it. The breath I took was shallow. An anxiety attack was suddenly upon me. My very being said run! If there was any doubt, the reptilian thing blinked … and then the dire wolf came to life. It shook off the slumber of death in anger. Snapped its jaws at the air and growled insanely at me.

I turned and slammed into what felt like a wall. "Aunt Trudy!" I screamed.

"I see the tea has done its work." She cackled at the words. Her eyes grew and focused on me.

"No … what?" I shouted.

"You'll make an excellent addition to the collection." She pulled a carving knife from her waist band and held it high over her head.

"You crazy hag!" I screamed and pushed her hard into the door I had entered from – what seemed only minutes before. She collapsed on the floor and began to jig and shake. Her noggin bounced on her shoulders like a bobble head.

While I was preoccupied with Aunt 'Psycho' Trudy, the animal heads came fully to life. When I turned, each of the monstrous creatures lashed and lunged and stretched its neck like a rubber band – out of the wall, right at me. The cabin began rapidly shrinking. Desperate for a way out, I ran into the first room I saw and slammed the door behind me. Seconds later the blade of the carving knife came through a panel of the door, followed by Aunt Trudy's diabolical laughter. "Right where I want you, Jon-ahhh-than."

The first thing I saw was a Windsor chair and I wedged its back straight up under the door knob. I turned, frantically looking for a way out. The window on the other side of the room would have worked, if it wasn't blocked by the crazy man Paolo from the forest and a giant Andean wolf beside him, ready to pounce on me and tear me to shreds. Each stood there with the same deranged, ferocious look as the creatures on the wall in the other room, except these two were not mounted to anything. I reeled back in shock and horror. But just as quickly, I realized they were unmoving ... eerily frozen ... they were ... stuffed?

"How do you like my work, Jon-ahhh-than?" She slammed her fists on the door, laughing insanely.

"You're not real," I shouted back at her. "This isn't real," I added. "Whatever it is, it's not real." I went to my knees. Pulled at my hair in frustration and lowered my head. "What did the barker say to me?" I whispered. "Just before I fell."

"Can't find your way home, kid?" a voice whispered nearby. "It's not for the faint of heart."

I raised my head, startled, about to shout.

"Ah, here you are, Jonathan," the woman beside me said in a slight Germanic accent. I was no longer in the cabin, nor was that Aunt 'Psycho' Trudy around. The woman speaking to me was a stranger, in her mid-fifties, a professional in a clinical way – meaning, she held a voice recorder and reached for a note pad from a nearby desk and placed it on her lap. She was buxom and blonde, sat in an armchair with her legs crossed. She looked tired. Her eyes looked glassy and swollen, like she hadn't slept in a while. It didn't bother me. I was chillaxin' on a day bed. Rather than listen to what the woman was saying, I oriented myself to the room. We were in a spacious office with dark paneled walls. A large mirror on the wall in front of me was set in an ornate, oversized gold frame. Other than that, paintings hung on the walls, large canvases of abstract art. Wide swaths of bright reds and pitch blacks, dark blues and blinding oranges, and other obscene hues along the rainbow. Patterns that lent themselves well to aggression or anger. It was as though a troop of howler monkeys on espresso had dipped their tails in paint and let loose across the canvases in a blind, frenzied, caffeine-induced jag. Or that maybe Aunt 'Psycho' had taken up painting to relax in her off hours. I found the works as unsettling as Brünhilde next to me. Any second, I half expected her to stand and sing an excerpt from the Götterdämmerung. Everything that had been happening to me the past several hours had been nothing less than unsettling. Why not add a little opera to the mix?

I was about to ask where the hell I was at when a loud knock on the door interrupted my thoughts. An attractive woman in a long, white lab coat entered. She was thirty or so, with dark hair and eyes. She carried a small black case in her hand, walked it over to the desk and placed it down.

"Dr. Bormann," the woman said. She had an American Southern drawl that made my ears perk. "I brought the case you asked for."

"Thank you, Sissy," the doctor replied. "You know Jonathan don't you, dear?"

"I surely do, Dr. Bormann," she replied. "How are you today, Jonathan?"

I probably should have kept my mouth shut until I figured out where I was and what the hell was going on. Instead, I reacted like it was a normal question under a normal circumstance that a normal person would reply to, and said, "I'd really like to know the answer to that myself."

Both women laughed at the remark.

"Has he been on the move again?" Sissy asked.

"All over," Dr. Bormann replied. "Haven't you, Jonathan?"

"I'm not sure I know what you mean," I replied. And I didn't. I didn't feel threatened by Dr. Bormann, and Sissy could stand next to me all day long.

"Jonathan just left his family's cabin in the Woods of Maine." Dr. Bormann was looking at me but speaking to Sissy. "Prior to that he was in Chile, high up in the mountains running from Nazis and Andean wolves."

"Legendary creatures, they say," said Sissy. "The wolves, not the Nazis," she grinned.

"We know the difference," Dr. Bormann said. "The Nazis who were in that colony ran torture camps – child prostitutes, drug rings, terror networks – you name it."

I stared in disbelief listening to the women speak. It seemed like days ago I had awoken in the forest and escaped. I thought of the man – Paolo – I heard his screams – it rattled my brain – the savage fury of the wolves tearing him apart, devouring him alive. I shuddered thinking of him, his fate ... and my own. Who were these people?

"Mercy me," Sissy breathed. "How frightening."

"We're getting close, Sissy," Dr. Bormann continued. "We were at the fair today, too. The barker and the pinwheel and that game of Karma."

"That was before the war," Sissy said. "Right?"

"Yes it was, which is why I think we're close."

"Close to what?" I asked. "Sorry to interrupt you two, but what?" Each woman looked at me like I was some kind of specimen.

"Was he on a magic carpet ride?" Sissy asked Dr. Bormann, ignoring me.

"Yes he was. Shooting across the galaxy," Dr. Bormann nodded.

"Well, bless his heart!" Sissy added with a comely smile.

I was parched and needed a drink of water. I didn't know where I was but I was done with these two. "Well ladies, it's been a pleasure," I said, and went to stand, except I couldn't move. My wrists, ankles, thighs, and chest were all strapped to the couch. "What the hell!" I snapped.

Dr. Bormann feigned a smile. "What do you think, Sissy?"

Without hesitation Sissy handed Dr. Bormann the small black case she had carried into the room. She nodded.

"I suppose you're right," said Dr. Bormann. "It's time." She opened the case and pulled a syringe with a six-inch needle extending from it. I went bug-eyed when she picked up a vial, drove the needle into it and loaded the syringe. She held the needle in front of my face and squeezed the syringe slightly. Just enough to watch the liquid spurt like she'd jerked off a mosquito. "This isn't going to hurt a bit," she smiled.

"Holy crap!" I yelled. "No! Are you two crazy?"

The two women looked at each other and laughed diabolically – just enough to convince me that they were. Dr. Bormann moved closer to me, and said, above a whisper," Actually, this is gonna hurt ... a lot."

"You could have said something about the war, Jonathan," Sissy said. "You could have told the truth!" Her eyes narrowed. That part sounded ominous. Everything about her was suddenly sinister, on the edge of psychotic.

"What war?" I shouted. "Because as long as I've been living, America's been at war. There's war everywhere all the time. Making people hate each other is big business. At war, wage war, kick start war – it's the biggest business on the planet. So tell me, 'What war?' Would you like me to pick one?"

She stared at me confused. "You don't even know – do you?"

Dr. Bormann placed the point of the needle to my neck – the jugular, to be exact. Tapped the vein with enough precision to draw tears to my eyes, but not penetrate the vein. "For someone who is so innocent you have quite the opinion of world affairs," she said. "So we'll give you one last chance. Do you have something you wish to tell Sissy?" she asked me.

"Look! I think you have the wrong guy," I said desperately, and winced at the pin pricks poking my neck. "Forget what I just said. I'm too young for war – any war. I'm a lover not a fighter."

"Are you really, Jonathan?" Sissy said. "Do you think Paolo would say that? Or what about your Aunt?"

"One I tried to help, the other tried to kill me! I defended myself."

"You're just about there," Dr. Bormann toyed with me, moving the needle, poking and prodding near the vein. She broke the skin, but did not drive it in, nor press the syringe. "But you're running out of time. Now, you better damn well tell me."

"I didn't kill them. I ran away. I escaped. Both were a couple of raging lunatics." I could say the same for them, and would have except for the six-inch needle that was on the verge of entering my jugular.

"What should we do?" Sissy asked.

"It's not my choice," Dr. Bormann replied. "Ultimately it's …"

"… Yes, I know, dammit, it's mine," I interrupted their little chat. "Ultimately it's my decision. I'll tell you what you want to know or what you want to hear. Just give me a little more time, will you? And I'll give you all I got." It was a passionate plea. I can give myself credit for that. Not that it meant much. It was honest, too. "Otherwise, I haven't a clue what you two are talking about, or for that matter, who you are or how the hell I landed here."

"That's very noble of you," Sissy remarked.

"The only problem is," Dr. Bormann continued, "I wasn't talking to you …" At which point, she pulled the needle from my neck and pressed a button on the desk. The large wall mirror across from me illuminated. The light revealed another room. People were inside it. Some, milling around, others sitting at workstations. They were of no consequence to me. The three that stepped to the window were. "… I was talking to them," Dr. Bormann pointed.

The three looked out on me – down on me – like gods standing atop Mount Olympus. Amidst the shock and terror of recognition, I had to wonder if they were gods. For they had surely played god with me.

"Where do we stand?" the man in the center spoke.

"Subject MK-Ultra 420B is, in my opinion, wiped clean," Sissy said.

"And what is you assessment, Dr. Bormann?" he asked.

"I concur with Dr. Hess, director," she replied as she gave a sharp nod toward Sissy. "420B has failed all experiential modifications of his environment, was undeterred by the perception management imposed, and was unresponsive in any way to the trigger, 'before the war.' As Dr. Hess just said, that is, in reference to his memory, 420B is wiped clean."

All three in the window nodded solemnly. Dr. Bormann continued, "In his mind, he is a young adolescent residing in a small community on the eastern frontier of Maine."

"You're telling me we've lost two decades of conditioning and perception management," the director asked calmly. "That the bubble's popped?"

"I'm afraid so," Dr. Bormann replied. "Unless …"

"… Unless what!" the director snapped.

"Unless the trigger was modified," she answered. "Then anything could happen."

"Dear God!" the director exclaimed. "We have no choice but to terminate this experiment." He looked to his left, then to his right. "Dr. Gertrude, Reverend Paolo?" My dear aunt and the redeeming pastor each nodded affirmatively.

"But you said it was a game," I shouted out to him. An all too familiar face from the get-go of this bizarre affair fixed its eyes on me. The entire room quieted. Everyone stared at me in disbelief, then slowly turned toward him.

"Karma is not a game, it's a way of life, kid," the barker said. "That's what I told you."

"You also said the pure of heart have nothing to fear."

"Ha! Well kid, do you?" His voice rose sharply at the question.

I breathed deeply and held it. I could feel my heart beating hard in the middle of my chest. I exhaled slowly, embraced a calm, and replied, "I have nothing to fear at all."

"Hmmm," the barker pondered what I said. He rubbed his chin and took the measure of the doctor and the reverend beside him – looked in both directions. If there was any hint on their faces at what action to take or how to proceed, it wasn't in any way noticeable. There was no nod of the head, nor slight gesture, not even a blink of the eye, by either. "Yes, indeed. It is a most delicate proposition. You are a subject of thought and condition. You have nothing; therefore, you have nothing to fear at all."

"Director Helms?" Dr. Bormann asked. She held up the needle for all to see. Her eyes fell on mine, hard and dark. No empathy or feeling in them, nothing there but listless chunks of Teutonic coal.

He nodded, and said, "We must compartmentalize, then, for a rainy day project."

"You realize he could go postal at any time – a shopping mall, a playground, a stadium, a carnival – if the trigger is truly modified," she said.

"You say that like it's a bad thing," he smiled. The doctor and reverend laughed.

"Let me further add, he cannot be directed to operate as needed against dissent – martyr an enlightened rock star or sanction a leader with ideals," she added.

My dear aunt then whispered in the barker's ear. "Yes," he said aloud. "Dr. Gertrude suggests we simply place him back where we found him, for another round of karma – another revolution around the sun." He cleared his throat. "I concur," and nodded.

"Very well, sir." Dr. Bormann did not hesitate. She stabbed the needle into my jugular. Jiggled it around, slowly injecting the vile toxin into me – into my brain. Within a matter of seconds, the center of my head began to burn. The fire spread down my spine to my toes.

"I told you it would hurt," she smiled and tapped my shoulder. "Just a little." Her grin went ear-to-ear. Not evil or wicked, that was the beauty of it. It was an ordinary smile. She could have been petting a dog or waving to a neighbor. Her sadism was total and complete.

"You bitch!" I managed to spit out. Choking on the words, I began to shake and spasm, and could speak no more. I wanted to tell her I would be back to find her – I'd find them all. But my thoughts ran wildly in my head – and just as quickly – withered. I tried to focus but could no longer function.

Silence then.

The world was dark.

For an age? An epoch lost?

Or a grain of time found? A moment? What does time mean?

Out of darkness came light, a starry web found me.

I was aware, in the present, in the midst of a galaxy, spinning and turning.

Like a pinwheel floating and spinning before my eyes.

The rotation slowed.

A fire in my head slowly burned out.

My thoughts were fuzzy, like I'd wandered in from a dream. I heard familiar sounds. There was laughter around me. An ox bellowed in the distance. A barrel organ played sporadically nearby. The barker was standing in front of me, slowly lowering the pinwheel and wand.

"You ready to play the game, kid?" he asked.

"Huh?" I mumbled. There was laughter in the crowd that had gathered in around me in front of the booth. "How long was I gone?" I snapped. "How old am I?"

"Gone?" the barker asked. "How old?" Everyone started to laugh and joke. "Kid, we haven't even started yet."

"I … I don't understand," I said. "I was somewhere."

"Sure you were – you were right here," he patted my shoulder, which was greeted with even more laughter from the rubes.

"Then what did you just say? Just a minute ago?" I asked him.

"About what?" he answered. "Your fate?"

"No," I shook my head, "after that."

"You mean, 'Never turn your back on monsters in a hallucination?'"

"Yes!" I shouted. "Why would you say that?"

At that, his face changed, his brow furrowed. His eyeballs seemed to swell out of their sockets. The harder he squeezed his brow the further his schnoz protruded from his face. He had thoroughly transformed into something serious and sinister. He leaned in and spoke slowly, "Because they might be your own." He glanced left and right, then quickly found my eyes again. He breathed deeply through his nostrils, and exhaled, "You don't wanna go postal? Do yah, kid?"

A man awakens in a cemetery and flees into the night. Mysteriously he walks into his past, toward a reckoning with a fiendish ghoul from his youth.

The Return of Mr. Poole

I hear a clock ticking, the precision of a metronome, back and forth. Steady. Rhythmic. The dream is upon me again. It's always the same. The veil draws tightly across my face, suffocating and blinding me. The laughter is childlike, faint and fleeting, and then a cackle of satisfaction and delight. I awake gasping for air and see it all afresh – the thing at the Noble house that day. Evil by any other name. I know, because when Dooley and I went running from my backyard over to the Noble's front yard, I saw it. The specter smiled at me. Lifted its hat and smiled with a slow nod, inviting-like, from up in the window of the room where poor Mr. Noble lay bleeding. I was pretty sure Dooley didn't or couldn't see the ghoul. That was my curse. I was the one who could see their kind. Dooley just stared at the insanity going on around us like he was trapped in someone else's nightmare. But not me. My imagination ran wild, and so did I. Every day of my life, until, when I could go no further, I finally fell. And I've been falling ever since, in a struggle to lift the veil.

I awake with a start and shake the dreamscape from my head. For a moment, I'm relieved it was only a dream. That is, until I stand. I feel disoriented and confused. I stumble around like a drunk, bracing myself against cold stone. A quiet expanse of meadow rolls under my feet. It's peaceful – much like a city park – a well groomed, manicured lawn – scattered with birch and maple trees. There's not a living soul around me. Why should there be? It's a cemetery, and I'm leaning against a headstone over a grave. I step back and take a hard look. It's freshly turned. The earth is dark, moist.

What the hell? I begin to panic. I can't remember anything but the dream. It's crowding my head. Dusk is passing and a crescent moon is low on the horizon, sputtering to rise. The first stars break through the twilight. I look around the field. But for the trees and headstones, it's empty, and as quiet as the marble and granite stones and slabs. There is no one here but me. Yet, I can't shake a creeping paranoia that some *thing* is here with me. When I break for the road, I do not turn back to look. If it's there, I don't want to see it. My pace quickens. Time wanes like an old moon.

The road is familiar enough. I quickly realize where I am, my old home town, up in the woods on the eastern frontier. A place the native Abnaki called Matagamon, literally meaning, "far on the other side." I reckon it was one of the few occasions white people listened to the natives, because the name actually stuck. The town is very small and located deep in the highland forest of Maine. Not to be confused with the Province of Le Maine in France, whence the name derives, but the state located on the Canadian border in the most northeastern corner of America. It's a wild, remote place – a frontier – one of the last frontiers that remain on the North American continent, to this day, in the post-industrial world. There is still forest primeval here, impossible to conceive, but so. Time here moves slowly, like dead water in a river, but it moves nonetheless. In the evenings, the heavens are brilliantly lit by a billion stars. The ebb and flow of the galaxy, the stream of the Milky Way, weaves its path above undiluted by the light of man, a light that pales in comparison, but is necessary. I can see all of that now – the stars above – the constellations that hold this grain of sand in their palm, carrying us through the stream. I never could before. In the days I walked the streets here I never looked up much. I placed one foot ahead of the other, one at a time, to just keep moving. I had to. It's the way a lot of people live here. The meaning of the frontier – the wilderness – is just that. It's not easily accessible. It's an effort to get there, and once you do it's an effort to get around, to survive and live comfortably. I think that's why the borders of the frontier have diminished so – to overcome the limitations nature places on man, the fear of the unknown, and the limitations man places on himself, innately. I've come to believe people in the modern age do not conceive of such places as the frontier beyond the idyllic. That is, if they conceive much of anything at all but the day-to-day path they walk. In this small town, like most places anywhere, the path most people walk is very narrow. They're just too damn busy. In my life, I've lived in many places, and traveled far and wide. There's only one place I grew up, however, and that's here on the frontier. The problem is – how the hell did I get here? I haven't lived here for thirty-nine years.

The sign post reads Pleasant Street. A wave of memory passes over me. I walk up the street. I pass the Taylor house, the Ames house, the Poulin house, and the Moore house – where my friend Dooley lived. All families I once knew. I come to the old Walker house and pass. On the porch I see the oldest son as plain as day, or a specter of him. But how? He shouldn't be alive. He was middle-aged then, when I knew him, or about him. He spent most days on the front porch rocker – rocking away – moving but going nowhere. His name was Henry, but every one of us kids called him Rocketman, on account of how hard he rocked himself like he was about to launch into orbit. Our parents told us to leave him alone – it was worth a smack side the head if any of us made fun, or were caught doing it. He had fought at Iwo Jima – had seen too much there – too much for one man to swallow. My father had told me that. Years later, I heard, after a childhood friend named Merrill came back from 'Nam, he too, acted similarly to Rocketman. Unlike Rocketman, one evening Merrill snapped and they took him away. They found him in combat gear walking down Main Street with a rake, thankfully, instead of an M-16, attacking cars and screaming "Charlie," at anyone who approached. He fell off the radar after that, and never did return to town. I mention this because it was then that I came to realize what Merrill and Rocketman had in common, or what they shared, and what my father had meant when he said it – what they had seen was too much for one man to swallow. They had never really come back. The part of them that worked, that functioned, was still there, with all the other lost souls, on the battlefield.

As I stare at Henry he stops rocking, stands abruptly, and points further up Pleasant Street, toward Willow Lane. I don't understand, but he begins to shoo me there, like it was where I needed to go, in that direction. As I do, he sits down and resumes rocking. The lane is a narrow, short alley of a street that dead ends about three-hundred feet in, where it backs into a playground for the grammar school. An older couple, the LaPointes, once lived on the street. We delivered newspapers to them for years – my older brother and I, who shared a paper route. Meaning, he gave me the houses that had all the big dogs. The LaPointes had a friendly pointer named Byrd that was prone to dry humping your leg. That was about it, so we took turns delivering the paper to their house. On Sundays we'd go together, because each Sunday morning they'd invite us in for breakfast – eggs, bacon, sausage, and pancakes, or French toast – all thoroughly soaked in pork grease. I never knew if they were childless or if their children or grandchildren were too far away, but they treated my brother and me like we were their own. Mrs. LaPointe doted on us, laughing and chatting, while Mr. LaPointe sat smoking a pipe in his plaid shirt and green work pants. "Never forget your roots," he'd say, nodding and smiling. The missus always wore a floral patterned dress of faded greens, reds, and yellows, under an apron stained in pork fat. She'd circle us, dropping food on our plates. I couldn't wait to be old enough to go to the grammar school, the sixth, seventh and eighth grade, so I could walk by their house each morning. But by the time I did enter the sixth grade, unfortunately, it was too late. Old man LaPointe's heart seized one morning while he was snapping one off on the crapper, and it wasn't long thereafter that Mrs. LaPointe had her stroke. Too much lard and bacon fat. Their arteries had turned to cement. I would think of them every now and then, over the years, and their generosity. The house is still there. Another family with children occupies it. But now I see the LaPointes, him in plaid, her in a floral dress and apron, on the front porch, chatting and laughing. Byrd is at their feet. They are there as plain as Rocketman Henry Walker was down the street. I wave to them. I want to tell them that I embraced a similar philosophy of being a good neighbor. But they can't see me, or so I think, until Byrd stands and points. I follow the dog's nose past me, to the street directly opposite me, across Pleasant Street.

I make an attempt to pull the pieces together in my head. What I know or can recall. I think of the freshly turned grave where I awoke. The eerie solitude of the cemetery. The presence there. Finding myself here in Matagamon walking the streets of what I once called home. I remember the headstone. The headstone. What the hell was the name on the headstone?

I go back to Pleasant Street, walking silently under the stars, and cross it. I come to Pearl Street. I turn, and when I do Byrd lays down. He curls up between the LaPointes, at their feet, and I watch the three of them evaporate slowly like a fog burning off in a morning sun. Pearl Street drops abruptly, steeply, and empties onto old Merrick Square. Near the bottom of Pearl Street lived a family, the Hargreaves. The family was poor and had many children. Two of them, Dave and Elaine, were around my age. Sometimes, we, the children in the neighborhood and the ones at school, would fight with them, or argue, or bully them. I could say that we knew no better, but we did. It was bad enough that they really were poor. But we had to add to their misery every chance we had or could. The reason eludes me. I run with a pack mentality without much conviction. I remember Dave as a bully, which didn't help Elaine's cause any, because she took the brunt of the abuse dished out by the kids he aggravated. She's in the front yard now, a child still, crying and bleeding, and ... desperate. I remember one day at school, Miss Wilson, an angry old hag who'd gone fallow years earlier, made

Elaine come to the front of the classroom. It was never a good thing to be called to the front of the classroom. Miss Wilson had a habit of patrolling up and down the aisles between the neatly uniform rows of desks, instructing pupils diligently and ruthlessly as she patrolled, gently tapping a ruler in the palm of her hand as she spoke. I imagined her as a drill sergeant at some time in her miserable life. She took great pleasure in smacking students with her ruler if their cursive was weak, or their artwork was sloppy, or their problem solving was incorrect. One morning, she snapped at a girl so loudly and suddenly, the child, ushered to the front of the classroom, wet herself in a prolific gush that drenched her panties, poured down her legs, and spread around the floor. That was tough to see. I did not escape the insanity of Miss Wilson, either. Once I failed to comprehend the elementary math equation of twenty-seven divided by nine equals n. I couldn't think. She stood over me breathing fire through her nose. My mind went blank, null, and void of anything but her ruler. By surprise, she grabbed me by the hair and slammed my head upon the desktop three times in succession, screaming "three!" with each blow. To the end of time, I think, I'll carry an aversion to math. I would find out much later that my mother had to be physically restrained by my father from beating the woman over the walnut she had planted on my forehead. To my mom's credit, no one was allowed to beat her kids. That privilege was reserved for her alone. It was just as well my mother didn't level her. Miss Wilson would not last that much longer. In the middle of the school year it was reported that she fell out of bed and broke her hip. She was actually drunk and caught her heel on a chair when she went to stand. She twisted, and then fell hard. They found her on her kitchen floor, broken and alone, in her self-loathing with her only companion – an empty bottle of gin.

That was my first encounter with karma, though I didn't know it at the time, and neither did poor Elaine Hargreave. Just a few days before Miss Wilson's demise, she made Elaine stand at her desk while Miss Wilson yelled at her for bringing lice into the classroom. All the while that Miss Wilson picked lice from the girl's scalp, she stammered with furious, cruel invectives as if Elaine carried the plague. I remember staring, with all the other students – stunned, frightened, and befuddled. At lunch time, however, we continued the assault on Elaine. I could tell you that we acted as we did because our teacher and role model acted the same way. You'd probably buy it, too. But get serious. We chased her, Elaine, all the way to her house – off the schoolyard, down Pleasant Street, down the steep ridge of Pearl Street, right into her yard. I was there, and Dooley was too, chasing her with a bunch of other dumb-ass ruffians. We yelled and shouted terrible things at her and about her. Elaine was fast – very fast. She had learned to run. But she was not as fast as me. I was the fastest runner in my class – in all of the grade school. And I was fast enough that day to catch Elaine, even with the head start she had. I caught her in her yard, stuck my big foot out and sent her airborne. We, the boys and girls who chased her, watched her fly and land in the gravel. I stood and laughed with the other children as she cried hysterically in humiliation and pain, scraped and bleeding. Later, I was deeply remorseful, and my shame was boundless. It bothered me for some time after. And though I did many things I regretted in my life, there were few that compared to the cross I bore for hurting that girl. The beating and grounding I got for that when my parents found out was pretty severe. I could say it covered all the other transgressions in my youth that I got away with. Even then, it didn't seem enough. It never has. She cries now, there in the yard, before me, the innocence draining from her like the blood flowing down her arms and legs.

I see a shadow pass behind her, but think nothing of it. I'm too moved. Moisture fills the corner of my eyes and I weep. My mouth moves silently and I whisper, "I'm so sorry," wishing I could somehow make things right. A moment passes, and she diverts her attention to me, nods approvingly, and says, "And I am free." With a wave of her hand, she indicates a heading, to the south. I wipe the tears from my eyes with the back of my arm. When I can focus again, she's gone.

My head hangs in shame as I walk south from Merrick Square as she directed. I go about a quarter mile, down outer Main Street, to

Forest Street. Another wave of memory strikes and shakes me free of Elaine Hargreaves. It's there, at number five, where I spent my first eleven years. The house was built in 1920, in the two-story bungalow style – the kind where the upper rooms thrust out of the roof, and dormers set out from them. A man stands in one of the windows. He's not really there for others to see, but I do see him, because, as I mentioned, I do see them. As a boy, I knew him as Mr. Sherman. That was the name I gave him, though he never told me his name. In fact, he never spoke. I think he lived here once, too, when he lived.

I look to the front room on the left, the bedroom where I was exiled in my youth. I had shared a room with my older brother until he 'picked up' the trombone. His 'playing' sounded like goats farting through aluminum foil. That's what I told him and anyone else who'd listen. And listen they did. At least my mother heard me. She decided I needed some space. Not my own space, but space from my older brother and his trombone, so she moved me in with my younger brother. There I spent my days and nights, on the bottom bunk bed, staring up at wooden slates that looked as sturdy as crusted hangnails. It was only a matter of time, I figured, before the sixty-eight pounds of boy meat came crashing down on me, crushing me like a cockroach, to my death.

The word makes me pause. By that age I knew about death, the word, anyway. A faraway aunt had died of cancer, and a great uncle had died of a heart attack. My great-grandfather had died in April of the year I was born. I knew all of these people from faded photographs and the memories shared. But in another way, death was all around me, sort of. For I could see what I came to know as ghosts. Ghosts like the aforesaid Mr. Sherman. He wandered the upstairs hallway and bedrooms of our house. Lost, I think, or maybe confused. But he knew I could see him, the prick, because he always came into a room to hang out for a while when I was in the room alone, or trying to sleep. It was how I realized I was different, too. None of my other brothers or sisters could see him. My parents thought I was nuts in that "boy's-got-a-helluva-imagination" way. I could see some features occasionally, but mostly, he was more shadow than a full-bodied apparition. So I named him Mr. Sherman after a chimney sweeper in town. Mr. Sherman, the ghost, was never mean or frightful. In fact, one time when I was really sick he came to my bed and watched over me all night. Other nights he came to tuck me in. He was not supposed to be real. There's no such thing as ghosts. That filled me with doubt, but what freaked me out the most was that nobody saw him but me. I would tell myself he was just a clueless dead guy, not a ghost. As I see him standing up there now, seemingly looking down on me, I smile and wave like seeing an old friend, but he does not return my greeting.

I wonder now if it's me. That he can't see me. Am I real? Is this moment real?

To my right, I see a star sparkle high over a house on the hill above. My attention is drawn there. The house is where the Smiths lived. Their house is older, built in the 1880s, when Forest Street was mostly farmland. It has a medium-sized barn attached to it. Actually, the barn was connected to a one-story garage that was connected to the house. My father said the house was a classic New Englander. I'm not sure what he meant by that, but I do recall the barn with all its chickens, which, compared to our chicken coop with its chickens, was like a palace.

I can see Mr. Smith on his porch, a sharpened axe in his hand. He calls for my father to lend a helping hand. I'm not sure why exactly, unless it was my father's job to ensure a steady hand to pour the whiskey. Such was the entertainment of my youth. I see myself racing to his barn and settling in the rafters with my friend Dooley and other children. Our legs swing freely. I watch Mr. Smith grab chickens randomly, place their heads over the rim of a barrel, and decapitate one after the other, blow after blow. He tosses headless chickens on the barn floor. It's not uncommon to see a chicken dance for minutes after it's lost its head. Soon, four or five headless chickens are running around bumping into each other. Throughout the whole affair, Mr. Smith whistles Amazing Grace. He pauses only to pound a short shot that my father hands him, and then goes right back to business. When the dance ends, each child receives two chickens – one for each hand –

to bring home to gut and feather. It is all nice and tidy, and a very efficient operation.

I always attributed that to Mr. Smith being an axe man. Comparatively, my grandfather, who kept an untidy chicken coop at our place, was not an axe man. He was a wringer. That was his preferred methodology, and, if truth be told, I'm pretty sure he enjoyed it. In fact, I'm pretty sure he hated chickens, claiming they were the dumbest creatures that walked the planet earth. When it came time to 'cull' our flock he'd show up at the house and yell, "time to wring the chickens," and lead the assault, grabbing one after the other with his bare hands and wringing their necks. He'd take them by the throat, and spin them around like a watch on a chain, and throw them over his shoulder to the ground. Bizarrely, they would not dance, but stagger around like drunks at a bar after last call, their little chicken heads drooping like limp dicks at a whore house on a Sunday night. The beheading would come later, after each and every one of them passed out for good, somewhere in the yard. My younger brother and I were charged to gather up the chicken corpses and throw them in a pile. Unlike Mr. Smith, my grandfather never whistled while he worked. He didn't have to. My older brother, from up in his bedroom, by then much improved on his trombone, would play Taps from his window, the bastard, mocking us while we picked up the carcasses.

Smiling at the memory, a memory I had long misplaced, my gaze falls upon the second floor again, and good old Mr. Sherman. "Who are you?" I say out loud. Incredibly, as if all I had to do was ask, I see him clearly for the first time. I'm stunned when I recognize him. It's my great-grandfather. His lips move. I hear no sound but the words form in my head. "Go," he says. "Find your way there, and you'll find your way back." He motions with his arm to Main Street, back toward town. Confused and bewildered, I nod goodbye, and leave Forest Street behind me. I trek up Main Street north past Merrick Square, toward downtown. I have a notion there's sordid business I must attend to. I pass the library, the police station, the county courthouse and jail, a bank, the town hall – things are picking up the closer I get to downtown proper. There are four churches – I'm sure there would have been five churches if there had been enough room – all of them Protestant – the Catholics were not allowed to build and worship on Main Street. Sensible people do not want them in the center of town, with the exception of them buying goods from sensible Protestant merchants. The *them* being mostly French Canadians or their spawn, and the spawn of Irish potato heads, the newer and the older immigrants to the town who work the mills, forests, and factories. You may think I'm cynical or outdated, but there are people who really do think that way – who practice social Darwinism. They do it with a smile on their faces, as if it's a joke, so it's all right to talk about that Frog or Mick anyway they want. The irony is they're the ones who've yet to evolve. The tragedy is they hold just enough resources to hold the rest of us back.

I know I'm nearing my next stop when I come upon the specter of Blethen's Grand Hotel. It lingers still, and that's nice to see, because it was an architectural gem, for these parts, from when it was built in the 1870s. I'm not sure how much time it has left. I imagine there are few left alive who entered there, myself included. When that time comes, when that last person passes, it will be gone forever. I discovered early on that the specter of inanimate objects can linger on for years after the object's destruction. It will not fully disappear as long as there is a soul living who has touched the object, that is, visited or held it. In this case, it's the hotel. It's been gone for thirty-nine years. A national chain store purchased the property and leveled the building the year my family moved from town. In its place a single story neo-Stalinist concrete block building was erected for the chain to sell its wares. In the building that replaced the Blethen, I see the architectural vision of the neo-Capitalist actuary and accountant is not that dissimilar from central planning in Stalinist Russia. In town, people soon forgot the Blethen was ever there, and went shopping in the new store. Forgetting is part of the genetic code of humans. It has to be. They forget who they are, where they came from, how they came to be, and the lessons learned along the way. People tend to live in the immediate and react or respond to that which only affects them, whether it be loss or gain. Sadly, the ghostly hotel is beginning to fade noticeably. I sigh. It won't be long before the last memory that holds it is gone, and the hotel fades completely. I swallow hard and think of my own mortality.

How is it I can see these things? Why is it still, I see and understand? And how is it I am here? Upon a summer night?

The bell of the Congregational Church interrupts my thoughts. It rings three times. At the third ring a memory charges through me like an electrical current. Blethen's Grand Hotel dissolves and I'm downtown, in front of the old phone company building. The first floor housed the operators. A job many considered one of the most important in town. At one time, they were the prime contacts and the main source of information for each town across the entire continent. The telephone operators controlled the flow of information, private and public, for each community. If you wanted to set your clock, you'd call the operator to get the "official" time. If you needed an address for a person or a business, you'd call the operator to get it. If you had to speak with someone the next town or state over, you'd call the operator to place the call. In big towns and cities, large pools of operators worked around the clock to keep the town connected to the world. But in Matagamon, on the frontier, it was remarkable enough that the phone company was one of three businesses open twenty-four hours a day, every day of the year, year after year. The other two were the county jail and the hospital. Unlike the other two businesses, the phone company staffed a single employee overnight, and that was an operator. A single person worked through the night to keep the town connected to the world. For people in the know, that was heavy, heady stuff. And I knew one of them. Actually, she was the mother of my friend Theodore Gardiner. Mrs. "G," we, all of us kids, called her. She worked the graveyard shift, which was from 8 p.m. to 6 a.m., three days on, three days off. I always liked Mrs. G, and I believed she liked us kids. I know she loved her family. I believe she did, very much. I remember her wearing a lot of makeup, even though she was a natural beauty, full-figured, with dark, shiny eyes and shiny hair as black as a raven. In one memory, I see her in the grocery store with Theodore and his sister, Louise. Her makeup was very heavy that day. They walked past me and my mother, who had stopped to speak with one of the old church ladies, Mrs. Lipton. After the Gardiners had said their hellos and continued by, Mrs. Lipton whispered, "That hussy," under her breath. I happened to hear it, but at that age, I didn't know what it meant. I think I was supposed to hear it, though, along with the other dozen people in the aisle. My mother, to her credit, rolled her eyes and pushed the cart onward, without another word to Mrs. Lipton. Later that night, I overheard her tell my father about poor Mrs. Gardiner, and how the woman needed to get out. I didn't know what she meant by that, either. She then said something along the lines of how could that old bag Lipton be that stupid. She was pretty angry – enough that her nightly quota of one glass of red wine was surpassed that evening by a full bottle.

In another memory, I see myself going to Theodore's house after school. Mrs. G had worked the previous night and was just waking at three in the afternoon. I saw her without her makeup for the one and only time. She walked into the kitchen where Theodore and I were sitting and talking. She had a black, bruised eye. Remembering how I once received a black eye when I walked into a door, I asked her if she'd done the same. I guess it was innocent enough, because she smiled, and came over and hugged me. I didn't mention the other time I received a black eye, when I got sucker punched by Steve Lambeau because I blew a kiss at his sister. A hug from Mrs. G – funny how some things don't let go. Her body was warm. When my head landed between her full breasts, my hope was it would get stuck there. She squeezed me tight enough that it almost did. My little pecker reacted like it never had before. It kind of throbbed and grew, as my belly went warm and tingly. She told me how important I was, and she'd never let go. That moment remained special to me. I suppose because of what became of her. I rarely went to the Gardiners' house. There was something there I didn't like. A feeling like the one that was coming on me now. I sense it's where this night is heading. It was suffocating, dark, and lifeless in that house. A shadow was upon it. A shadow, I fear, that is still nearby.

I think of Mrs. G now as the last chime from the Congregational Church's bell fades. It's time. The bell hath tolled. The man-like dark figure comes from the side of the building. It carries something in its hand. It looks like a baseball bat. It walks past me as though I am not here. It's enough that I wonder if I really am. The dark figure strolls up the sidewalk to the phone company building. I see it take the stairs one step at a time – slowly, methodically, deliberately – and then approach the door. It's locked, but it needs no key – this time. It pauses, and then passes through the door. I hang my head in sorrow. It is but an echo, but the scream within is agonizing. The words, "Why?" "The children!" and "No! No!" are shrill and desperate – the last words Mrs. G ever speaks. It is 3 a.m. on Thursday morning, June 25, 1964, when it happens. I never forget the date. In fact, over the years I come to know much about that date. Irrelevant stuff like, in 1630, the table fork is introduced to American dining by Governor Winthrop of Massachusetts. Which meant, from that time forward, the behavior of the Puritans would be considered barbaric in deed only. In 1835, the first building in Yerba Buena, Spanish for "good and plentiful grass," is constructed. The place is California. The town is renamed San Francisco. A cosmic alignment begins. In 1876, George Armstrong Custer and the 7th Cavalry are wiped out by Sioux and Cheyenne warriors at Little Big Horn in Montana. People ask how a bunch of technologically inferior savages with high cheek bones, sloping foreheads, and squinty eyes could defeat a technologically superior race of Anglo-Saxon warriors? The strongest army on earth? They ask the same question a hundred years later, and get the same answer. But because of the genetic predisposition of the subjects who ask the question, they forget, and are doomed to repeat the same mistake time and again. In 1938, Ella Fitzgerald and the Chick Webb Orchestra hit number one in the charts, with "A Tisket A Tasket." Nine years later, in 1947, the first edition of Anne Frank's, The Back of House, is published. If there were any doubts the Germans were not going to hell, they are obliterated now. The Spanish, French, English, Austrians, Russians, and Ukrainians sigh in relief. They are finally off the hook for the previous millennium of recreational pogroms, death, and destruction against the Jews and Jewish culture. Three years after that, the Korean 'Conflict' starts when North Korea invades South Korea. It has yet to be resolved. In 1954, Joseph Montague O'Malley is born. Ten years later, on that morning, Mr. Gardiner takes a leisurely stroll from the phone company back to his house, all the while laughing hysterically and swinging a blood-stained baseball bat that he's just bludgeoned his wife's head with. There, in the kitchen where I once sat, he finishes the bottle of whiskey he'd started earlier that night. The gas stove is on, but the burners are not. At 4 a.m. he lights a cigarette and blows himself to hell.

Theodore was at my house that night. He and four other friends were celebrating my tenth birthday. Fortunately, Louise was sleeping at a friend's camp out on the lake. That was the only good news that went around town for the next several weeks. I would lose my friend, Theodore, however. He and his sister went to live with Mrs. G's parents in Bar Harbor, then Boston, and then San Francisco. They finally went to Maui, I heard – far enough away to co-exist in peace with her memory.

I ponder again. What did my great-grandfather mean? Find my way there, I'll find my way back?

Yet, the evening is beginning to coalesce, at least my thoughts are. All the memories are flooding into my head. All but one. I think of the cemetery and how I arrived there. My mind is blank. I continue down Main Street, thinking what to do next, where I'm going, not sure if I'm being pushed or pulled, and ... by who or what. I pass a bank, Leo's Drug Store, three department stores, Bickmore's Barbershop, The Center Theater, and cross the Mooselook River Bridge to First National Grocery, then right past the Esso gas station, and Bob's Feed and Grain. But for Bob's, every one of those shops and storefronts are either ghostly apparitions or vacant, empty shells of the prosperity that once was.

For some reason, I turn right at Bob's Feed and Grain on to Lincoln Street. The street is lined with big houses. A handful are borderline mansions. Most of the houses on the street date from the late Nineteenth and early Twentieth Century, though a few remain from the 1820s and 1830s. There's one, even, left from the late Eighteenth Century, dating from 1796. It's called the Blood House. I remember how folks would say George Washington was president when Rufus Blood and his family moved in. The joke being it was the only house George never slept in. Though everyone still called the house – an oversized two-story Cape with a central chimney – the Blood House, no Blood had lived there since 1873.

I walk up to the house. It shows its age. It's fallen into disrepair. The windows are dark. Some are broken. Clapboards are loose and swing freely. Others have fallen to the ground. A great horned owl is perched atop the remains of a partially collapsed chimney. The owl hoots loudly. Its cry is foreboding. Many bricks are scattered on the roof. The yard is as unkempt as the house. The grass is knee deep and the driveway has gone to weeds. Two birch trees in the yard reach to the sky. They stand rigid like sentinels over a tomb. It saddens me. It always does when I look upon the Blood House. After the last Blood moved out of the house, the property turned over several times. In the 1960s it came into possession of a family named Leighton. He was a pilot for Pan Am and traveled frequently. His son, Will, was a year younger than me, but we played on the same little league team. Captain Leighton was a part-time coach. He knew the game well, and had even played college ball. He made me a catcher and I played that position through high school. But he was gone too much to coach fulltime. The slack was picked up by his good buddy, Sheriff Marck, who was the head coach. Will was a good pitcher. I remember him throwing hard for an 11 year old. His little sister and mother came to all the games and cheered us on. His sister was cute, and was on her way to looking like her mother, a bona fide goddess. She was a former stewardess for Pan Am, it was said, which is how the Leightons met. She was also a big-chested, slim-waisted blonde. We all took notice of that. Every boy quieted whenever she came in the dugout to bring water or drop oranges for the team. Our little heads would pop up like gophers on the lonesome prairie in her presence. During the two seasons I played baseball with Will, I made an extra effort to play catch with him in his backyard just to catch fleeting glimpses of his mom. Their yard was big enough for catch, and there were lilac bushes along the property line to keep the ball in play in the event of a wild throw. Later, I'd always think of Mrs. Leighton when I caught the scent of lilac wafting on a late spring breeze. I see her now in one of her tight sweaters walking across the lawn slowly, coming toward me, smiling seductively. She carries a pitcher of lemonade or something. I can almost touch her, and when I go to do it, her smile fades and her face is frozen like plastic, but it's translucent and sinister. I gasp, and she dissolves into dust.

By now, you're probably asking yourself if I had a thing for my friends' mothers, or maybe just older women. I was just a kid, Homer – a kid who saw too many things – things no one else could see, things he probably shouldn't have seen, things he wasn't supposed to see, or for that matter, he didn't want to see. I'd like to ponder the racks on Mrs. Leighton and poor Mrs. G, I really would, just as much as I'd like to steer this macabre stroll down memory lane away from where it is taking me. I would, but I feel the night slipping away as rapidly as my life …

… Ah, my life … My memories … These particular memories … They're coming at me hard … and to a head.

The lilac bushes are gone now. When I walk up to the house, I see him there, in the front parlor. Waiting or watching, or maybe both, I'm not sure. In a world of possibilities, I question how it came to be. I was 13 that autumn when word came of the accident. How tragic it was. Sheriff Marck was up for re-election that November. A well respected and trusted man, he had served three terms, and was set to be elected by the voters for a fourth. That was, until the accident, deep in the forest off Mountain Road, near Parson's Drop, when he went hunting with Captain Leighton and mistook the Captain's head for that of an eight-point buck. It was a terrible hunting accident, the coroner ruled, and a very sad affair. So much so, that Mrs. Leighton was near crumpled to pieces until that day, some six weeks after the burial,

Sheriff Marck moved into the Blood House. The following Tuesday he lost the election. By Thanksgiving, he, Mrs. Leighton, and the children, had left, moved to Augusta where they settled. Sheriff Marck was appointed deputy warden in charge of firearm safety for the State Fish and Game. The Blood House has sat empty since, some forty plus years. Try as they might, no real estate agent could sell the house. No one would buy it. No one ever will. I think it's because of him, Captain Leighton. Occasionally, he'll pace in front of the bay window impatiently, but mostly he sits and stares ahead blankly. I wonder ... does he know what's happened? Does he know they're never coming back? That they're gone?

From Lincoln Street, where I stand, ahead of me, the street splits. I take a few steps, but I 'm not sure where to go. I take one last look at the Blood House. The Captain is in the window, looking in my direction. Does he see me, too? Or is he looking through me? I am not surprised when, just as I'm about to turn away, he raises his hand and points. I follow the end of his finger to a sign post that reads Davis Street. I nod, understanding, and, incredibly, he responds with a wave as the darkness consumes him. I come to the street and turn on it. It's narrow and hilly, but I don't mind. I'm trying to connect the dots as I walk. My memory drifts. I see them all – Henry, the LaPointes, Elaine, my great-grandfather, Mrs. G, Captain Leighton – and I think – they have pulled and pushed me here to this end, on this night, for one purpose. It's as though they have eased me in.

I chance upon the stars. The night is late. It is not long till first light. I suddenly become aware. I must have full resolution. Otherwise none of this will matter. It will mean nothing. My life – this life. I reach the top of Davis Street and pause. I have to. It's rushing at me – the dream – the veil slowly lifting. There, the next street over, I see where this night must end, finally, for us all – on Union Street. I do not want to go down the street – down there to that house. Not now or ever. And it's all because of what happened there, a July day, one Sunday afternoon.

When I was twelve, my family moved to a larger house on Davis Street, which is one street over from Union Street. Our backyard almost touched Union Street. It was big and spacious – nearly two acres – all of it mowed, with the exception of a few apple trees and a small vegetable garden my mother had planted. Our house is still there, but filled with strangers. They do not know what happened. What began there. Like our smaller house on Forest Street, the house on Davis Street had an occupant. Unlike our old house, the thing in the new house was dark – something very malignant. From the day we moved in, I sensed it. I knew where it was, upstairs, in the back room on the left, what became my bedroom. I told my folks they'd made a big mistake moving here, but they ignored me or didn't believe me. Who could blame them? I didn't understand how the world worked then. People need to feel the burn to believe how hot the fire is. It's human nature. The months of suffocating nightmares, the pockets of frosty air, the slow turn of the closet doorknob, the push of the door, the ink black shadow man – none of that mattered to them. It took a cure for my father's constipation for him to believe me. That's what he said the night he caught the image of the thing in the corner of his eye – right in the mirror. It stood behind him, menacingly, with a raised arm. I know, because I caught a glimpse of it, too – a nasty, foul thing – a face ghastly pale, as much the plastic as Mrs. Leighton's face, with black hollowed eyes and a thick, heavy moustache. Its black suit and wide-brimmed fedora were from another era, like in the pictures I'd seen of my grandfather as a young man. I thought the thing was about to strike my father with its raised arm. It had stepped from the ether directly behind him as he was putting me to bed. He was rubbing my head, as I was pleading with him once more how frightened I was to be in the room. He was telling me again that I was twelve years old, and that I needed to start acting like it. Besides, he was in the next room over. Thinking about it, I believe its intention was to show itself to just me. It wanted me. The thing knew I was isolated and vulnerable by my father's words. But when my eyes bulged out of my head, my father caught the reflection of the thing in my dresser mirror. Instead of striking my father, it lifted its fedora from its head and cracked a wicked smile that would have shattered the heart of a weaker or older man.

The top of its head, the crown, was missing – blown off by a shotgun blast. Even I knew the only possible way to create that type of wound was by placing a shotgun barrel in its mouth.

That moment creeps by even now.

Jolted, my father spun around as it dissolved into the ether from where it came. He grabbed me, took me from the room immediately, and slammed the door shut behind us. He made it to the bathroom, as I mentioned, and took the cure. He was shaking and cursing wildly at or for the saints. When he came out of the bathroom, he and my mother talked, or, my father blathered and my mother listened, nodded occasionally, and gasped frequently. My name was mentioned more than once, in connection with her grandfather and some aunt I didn't know. They attempted to make sense of it all. When my mother finally did speak up, it was only to say that what the neighbors had told her about the room was true. A wicked man named Poole had killed himself in there thirty years before. Both of them nodded. They apologized to me for not believing what I had said, and for putting me through the ordeal because of it. They told me they were foolish, and I was very brave. The next day, the room was emptied by my mother with help from the neighbors who had told her about the man named Poole. I moved back in with my younger brother, into the bottom bunk. The door to Mr. Poole's room was shut and locked – like that was gonna keep the thing inside.

Weeks later, I came home from school and our priest, Father Cox, was leaving the house. He looked a little flush and visibly upset. He said my name, "Joseph," and nodded, and placed his hand on my shoulder as though to comfort me. When he did, something caught his attention, ahead of him, off to the right, behind me. He jumped in fright, and rushed on without another word. I didn't know it then, but he had the same desperate look in his eye that I would see years later in the eyes of people whose imagined order of the universe is instantaneously and unmercifully shattered by truth.

I found my mother in the kitchen, smoking a cigarette nervously. She said she had to speak with me, to confide in me, tell me why Father

Cox was there and what had happened. Up till then, my experience had taught me that adults went to great lengths to exclude children from the breadth and depth of their world – narrow and shallow as it was. Nevertheless, she said that she and my father had asked Father Cox to bless my room. She called it "my room" because, even though I never wanted anything to do with the room because of the dark thing that haunted it, and even though I would never step a foot in that room again as long as we lived in the house, it was forever referred to as my room.

My mother stared at me. Buried in thought. She put out the cigarette. Actually, she mashed the thing into the ashtray repeatedly, and then quietly lit another. She told me her grandfather had an eye. So did my Aunt Elizabeth – have the eye. I did too, she confessed. My parents knew it from the time we lived in the Forest Street house, from the things they heard me say to what she and my father called my "imaginary friend," which I now knew was my great-grandfather – her grandfather. She finished the cigarette, and mashed that one repeatedly too – I think to muster up the courage to confront the beast, for I'm sure that's what it was. It had taken a lot out of her, as anyone. She nodded toward the stairwell, and said, "Follow me. I've something to show you." My mother led me upstairs to the bedroom. The door was open and so was the window. It faced the backyard. Through it, I could see the Noble house, the front of it, directly in the distance, over on Union Street. As I said, I never stepped foot in that room again, so I looked from out in the hallway. When my mother asked, "Do you see it?" I replied, "the Noble place?" She shook her head no, and pointed to the window sill. My eyes laid sight on what looked like claw prints scorched into it. Hanging, or clinging, from the outside-in, burned into the wood. It looked like someone had grasped it, the sill, before they slipped and fell. There was nothing more to say. I understood.

Later that evening, over tea in the kitchen, I heard her explain to father that when Father Cox blessed the room with holy water, it made a momentary hiss like steam from a kettle. The smell of burning wood suddenly filled the room, but there was no smoke or fire. Just as mysteriously, as the burning-wood smell evaporated, the scorched prints materialized on the sill. My father let out a low whistle. Weeks before, he had been a different person. He had always gone to church Sunday and prayed to God daily. He believed in a heavenly afterlife – something along the lines that most hominids share and imagine – a blissful hierarchy of angels, saints, and a carefully constructed bureaucratic ideal of unbridled entitlement. That was heaven – no strings attached. But then and thereafter, he was forever, and until his dying day – his passing – a philosopher. There really was more to heaven and earth than what is known, he realized. There was an in-between, a twilight world of infinite possibility, light and dark.

As for Father Cox, I'm not so sure. By the following Sunday service, he'd changed.

"He's only 48 years old," my father said to my mother, shaking his head in disbelief. It was right after mass. We were driving to my grandparents' home for Sunday dinner. "It simply can't be!" But it was.

"He's been relieved, not transferred," my mother replied. "He told the archdiocese about the blessing – about what happened – what he witnessed."

"They don't believe him?" My father yelled out incredulously.

"He said it wasn't a matter of faith for him to decide, but a matter of stability for them to decide."

"All they have to do is look at him," my father said with disgust.

True. Since Wednesday, when I had seen him walking out of our house and away from me, Father Cox had changed, visibly. More than frail or harried – although he was both of those things. His eyes were red and swollen, and showed the signs of worry like he hadn't slept in five days – like he was fearful and nervous. From that I came to realize that most talk a good game about their divinity – whatever their belief. They hold onto it right up to that day when it's just you – your own mortality – and it – doubt – that moment when all faith crumbles like a sand castle under a tidal wave – the one last nanosecond between eternity and oblivion. But what if you found out beforehand that divinity entails more than what you've been told and what is known? What then? My father had been able to reconcile that question when he saw the thing. Did that make him stronger than Father Cox, who was unable to? I say that because of Father Cox's hair, which had gone the color of bleached flour – stone-ground white – in a matter of days. In the business of religion, like in all business, success is determined as much by perception as performance. Even when Father Cox did get his wits about him, he never was or looked the same, which was not good for the image that the Church must maintain. No matter how well he could perform, he had seen too much that day at our house.

As I walk up Davis Street, I weigh and wrestle with the past. The flow of memory is upon me fully. I'm in the backyard of our old house, pacing and looking directly at the house on Union Street as I do. I can see the children, the family that lived there when I lived here, the Nobles. There were many of them. I recall two sons and four daughters. One of the sons was my age. His name was Roland. We were friendly, but not that close. I liked sports, and music, and reading. He liked cars, and engines, and mechanics. We both liked wildlife and would occasionally hike the forest paths in hopes of glimpsing a deer or moose or whatever else we saw, or sometimes go rabbit hunting. Just being in the forest was adventure enough, if you believe in such things. There are times I wondered what happened to Roland, his brother and sisters, and his mom. I wonder that if we had truly beaten the thing in my bedroom, the back room on the left, if things would have or could have turned out differently. I am only one soul. Even now, I look at a billion stars above. I know there are a billion more behind them, and, behind them, and so on. Heavy shit to wind the mortal coil, if you're so inclined. What does it matter now? I think of one thing. I think of Roland's father that Sunday afternoon in July those many years ago. Why did the son-of-a-bitch, after Sunday dinner, sneak upstairs and quietly stick the shotgun in his mouth and pull the trigger?

I have said that death was around me, which it was and is. It's around all of us constantly. It hovers – waiting. But in those days, we had time to pause and reflect about death. That finality. I could not imagine then that death could be viewed as a box score from yesterday's baseball game. Given but a glance before the page is turned, or that it could sell advertising, cheap fodder on local and the cable news where it is presented hourly, impersonal and without context, for its macabre entertainment value. In those days, when death happened, everyone in town reflected on it. It was as profound as the birth of a child – everyone had a stake in it. You felt connected – you felt a part of it. Me, for my part, I felt more than most in town, and saw more, too. I reflected on the thing in that room I had slept in – whatever it was – and when it was cast away from that room did it drift to Union Street, to the Noble house? And if it did, could it have planted a seed in the head of old man Noble? Could it have stood behind him repeatedly? Terrorized him in so many ways? As it had terrorized me?

Fuck!!! I don't want to go over there.

I don't want to own what happened there in 1966. I was a kid. A child. I didn't know anything. I didn't know it was possible. I was in the backyard playing catch and shagging fly balls with my friend, Dooley Moore, when the blast shattered the front window on the top floor. The glass went flying out onto Union Street. Moments later I heard the children start to scream. I saw the family run frantically out of the house and into the front yard, running in circles, shouting hysterically, and pointing to the second floor. I still did not know what possibly could have happened. How could I? My life was baseball, the stars above, and everything in between.

Dooley and I – me with my mitt, him with his bat – stopped and gawked. "What happened?" Dooley said.

"Dunno," I replied. "Let's go see." The spectacle before us was profound and surreal. The shrill screams of agony and sorrow filled the neighborhood.

"I don't think we should," he said. "Something's very wrong. We should wait."

"Wait for what?" I said. "Maybe we can help."

We ran over. Confusion was mounting. The screaming was hysterical. We got there and the realization exploded like a concussive blow to the head. Like the one Mr. Noble self-inflicted.

Dooley was right, but it was too late.

When you're a kid and you see your friend's father's splattered head parts come out of his house in a plastic bag, resting on the chest of his body that is being wheeled out on a gurney stretcher, and you know the guy was sane as the rest of us who, by choice or birth, live on the frontier, and you know what had happened to you weeks before, the nightmarish thing in your bedroom that had cured your father's constipation, and that your mother and priest had banished it from the bedroom you had inhabited, that they had exorcised it and, in all probability, had cast it directly toward the Noble house, then you might feel as I do.

The guilt of a thousand generations.

A pox upon me – oh, by the *what if?* of history, and its mighty weight.

You know now what happened when Dooley and I went running into the Nobles' yard. How that thing spotted me from the second floor window, the same room where poor Mr. Noble laid still and bled out. It caught my gaze and waved like we were old friends. It then lifted its hat and laughed, pointed at me, and waved for me to come. "I want more," it hissed.

It's not what happened next that mattered, but what happened after. How the story of my life turned on that moment, just as I turned when I felt Dooley's hand on my shoulder, and ran right into him and his baseball bat as it swung around. He had turned hard while the bat rested on his shoulder, and looked up at the window. In the split second before the bat connected, I caught the look in Dooley's eyes, staring and gaping at the window in holy terror as the thing pleaded for more. And that's when it struck me – just as hard as Dooley's baseball bat struck my head in the same instant – what Dooley and I heard and saw and what I finally understood – who it really wanted – not "I want more," but "I want Moore."

Oh no! "Shit! Shit! Shit!" The name on the headstone! "Dooley Moore! Oh! Dooley, why didn't we stay in my yard? Why didn't I listen to you?" I scream out.

I wanted to warn him, but I could not speak. The blow

overwhelmed me. I staggered and stumbled ... I fall for what seems a great distance, away from the world, past all those I've known and know – the old and new, the secret lives, the buried past, the passage of time, guilt and shame, and into the web of darkness ...

... The veil is lifted.

"Joseph." A faraway voice calls my name. "Joseph." It says again, but closer, and tells me I will remember everything. I do, and open my eyes. A gray twilight approaches in the west. The clock that was ticking like a metronome has fallen silent. Out the window, I hear a bird screech, and then another screech louder. A dog growls, barks loudly, and then whimpers in submission. I'm groggy, sweaty, and slightly nauseous. I gather my wits. My head aches – deep in the lobes – a dull, steady throb. I wonder how long I've been down and out.

"Joseph?" The voice asks calmly, soothingly. "It's me, Doctor Navarro." He is gently tugging my arm. "Joseph, it's Mike!"

"Mike?" I say.

"Are you all right?" he asks.

"Yes, I think so," and I raise my head from the day bed, orient myself, get my bearings.

"Can you focus?" He is sitting by me in a leather chair.

"You mean in my head or my eyes?"

"Each, I suppose," he smiles and reaches for a glass of water that was waiting on a table under the window. "Here," he says. "You must be parched."

I nod slowly. He is right. My tongue is bone dry. I've been speaking for a while, I suppose. I sip at the water, and then down it all. My head spins, flaying at making sense of what happened, what I recalled.

"Very good." He turns to a nearby video camera, mounted on a tripod, and speaks into it, "This is Doctor Miguel Navarro. The time is 17:52, 19 October. Patient: O'Malley, Joseph M., is now fully alert, hypnotherapy session successfully terminated." He reaches over and stops the recording. "That was quite a session, Joseph."

"All too real."

"You found your way there."

"They took Dooley away on a stretcher, I remember that."

"Yes, Joseph." He lifts the camera off the tripod and holds it. "It was very traumatic – too traumatic for such a young boy."

"How I wished I could have saved him."

"But he hit you in the head with the bat."

"Not on purpose."

"Some say it was, like he suddenly went mad."

"I think the word is 'possessed'."

"The trauma, the shock of what you witnessed."

"Come on, Mike."

"It was traumatic enough for you, Joseph. Considering where they found you, later."

"I had a moment. That's all. I ran away. Had to."

"You ran away? They found you face down on Dooley's grave. You gave everyone a good scare."

"I was paying my last respects."

"You were at the funeral. He'd been buried for days."

"I was responsible for his death, okay!" I shout. "I made him go over there. He didn't want to, but I made him."

"Anger isn't going to help, Joseph," he says as he begins to fidget with the camera.

"It's more like frustration, Mike," I sigh. "I'm too tired of no one listening or believing – tired of telling people there are ghosts, and some of them are not very nice."

"If that's true, as you say, that you can see them, then now might be a good time to make peace with Dooley." He twists up the corners of his mouth into a mock ghoulish smile.

"Don't patronize me, Mike. I'm dealing with a lot of shit here."

"You're right, Joseph," he replies. "As your friend, I apologize. I didn't mean to be insensitive. As your therapist, it was very unprofessional." I give him a nod. "I can honestly tell you that you are perfectly sane and normal by any standard, with one exception – and that is in your insistence about all this ghost business and how you are haunted by a thing."

"Are you recording again?"

"No, rewinding a bit." He looks up and smiles at me. "I want to show you something." He stops the camera, shakes his head no, and then hits rewind again. "Some people are not susceptible to hypnotic suggestion, Joseph, and honestly I did not think this would be helpful for you. I know remembering such a thing isn't easy, but I think you made a breakthrough today."

"What? That I can now remember the look on my best friend's face?" I reply. "The moment he was literally scared to death?" I say.

"The coroner's report said it was shock – at what he had seen."

"The ghoul? Oh, yeah. But that's what happens when it gets close and people get close to me. That's when it happened to my father and poor old Father Cox. Dooley freaked, that's what happened, when he touched me. Then he could see it too. That's when it showed itself."

"Yes, he freaked out, which was understandable." He stops the camera, takes a sharp breath, and breaths out slowly, "But ... you ... didn't."

"No," I pause, wrapping my thoughts around the beast – the memory – that I just tethered to a pole in my head, "because I ..."

"... can see things," he finishes the sentence, but he says it as if he is convincing himself. "You were ready – prepared in your own way. He wasn't. Who the hell would be?" He studies the screen on the camera as he speaks, then looks away. He places it down, takes a deep breath and exhales, unsure of himself. Seconds pass in silence. He pulls his watch from his pocket, checks the time, then places it on the table, near where he'd placed the camera.

"What? Did you find what you wanted to show me?" I ask. He says nothing. He glances over at the camera on the table again, but quickly averts his eyes from it. "I asked you not to patronize me, Mike." But he does not respond. He leans back in his chair, becomes restless, if not perplexed. Something is wrong.

"What the fuck!" I pick up the camera from the table realizing – all too late – what has happened. Over the years I have learned to co-exist with my third eye. I have learned to shut it, as it were, and open it, at will. I've told very few people about it. Why bother? They don't believe you. They mock you and laugh at you. Though, when you tell them their Uncle Paul said to smarten up or he'd throw you off the top of Borestone Mountain like he did your baseball cap, or that your Grandmother Harriet tells you she's the one who stepped on your playhouse, crushing it, not your sister, then they shut down. Back off. Become suspicious, and then afraid. After all, Harriet and Paul have been dead for decades. It's impossible for me know such things. Blah! Blah! Blah! I've become so sick of it – all but for one thing. These past few years, what had happened to me growing up on the frontier haunted me – the things I did and what was done unto me. I wanted closure. I reached out to my old friend from college, Doctor Mike, a successful psychiatrist these days. He knew me, and what I could supposedly do. "Parlor tricks," he'd always said, "Very impressive!" and left it at that. After months of sessions, he finally suggested hypnosis. So today I went under, and honestly, there were times I didn't think I would find my way out. Vivid memories, too fucking vivid. It never occurred to me that when I was out, my eye would open on its own. But open it did.

I look down at the camera screen and then back at Doctor Mike. His face has turned the color of grayish, earthen clay. I look back at the camera screen, the frame where he'd stopped rewinding. It was the moment he'd tugged my arm. He was calling my name, to bring me back, while ... touching me. Can it be ... when I returned ... I was not alone? The proof is in the picture ... at the window ... frozen in that single frame ... there he stands.

Outside, I hear a faint laugh, distant, but close enough. It cackles with satisfaction and delight, knowingly. Dear God, it really is him, and he's found his way back.

I shudder at the thought ... at the horror.

Mr. Poole has returned.

*Demonic spirits compete with an angelic visitor to
claim a murder victim in his final moments.*

Prelude to a Storm

The man leaned back in his armchair slowly, nervously. A revolver, the barrel of which could have housed Lou Gehrig's baseball bat, was inches from his face. So close, the odor of its oily residue filled his head. He could pretty near lick the damned thing. That option was not on the table, however – he wasn't holding the gun. That would be one of the two men who had crept into his front parlor – somehow – where just moments before, he sat alone reading the newspaper, taking sips from a glass of Scotch whiskey and gently puffing a cigar. They had come into the house, without warning or invitation, under the cover of darkness and an approaching storm. Opened and shut the parlor door without notice. He had lowered the paper to take a sip of whiskey and they, and the gun, were there. Fear, sudden and complete, rushed through him. The paper slipped out of his hands. The cigar fell from between his lips,

First published as the opening segment of the 2017 John Derhak novel *The Guardian Angel of Death*, a supernatural thriller set in 1930s coastal Maine. Reprinted here as a freestanding story. For information about the book, see johnderhak.com.

153

bounced off his lap, and onto the floor. He wavered on the brink. In all certainty, he was fit to shit himself. The great Houdini could not have conjured such magic so dramatically to such an end.

Ah, the end.

The evening was late. The radio had signed off and he had been minutes from bed. The headlines in the paper had been of little interest to him. A depression was on and a fella named Roosevelt was running for president. Another man, Brann, a Maine Democrat, had just won the governor's seat. That bode well for the fella named Roosevelt. In a matter of weeks, he'd find out if it was true, the old adage, "As Maine goes, so goes the nation." The Association Against the Prohibition Amendment had held a rally in Bangor Tuesday. Roosevelt had pledged to end the social experiment. Yet, politics and the economy didn't matter to the man in the chair. His interest had been drawn to a pair of stories on page three. The two men shot dead in a Cape Cod warehouse in August were related to illegal smuggling, one story had read. The other story had been closer to home – the waning coverage of a local fisherman whose body had floated in on Moose Harbor. The blow to the head must have resulted in the fall overboard, the coroner had determined, rendering him unconscious, which resulted in the fisherman's drowning. But what caused the blow to the head?

He had been so engrossed with the latter story, he had not heard a thing except the sound of distant thunder and the wind, which, he now realized, had betrayed him. It had rattled and rocked the old house, muting the sound of their entry. He glanced from one man to the other and back at the gun barrel. The two before him were in long, dark overcoats, and they stared menacingly from under the brims of dark fedoras. The scene was eerie and frightening, and another wave of fear rushed at him.

Never one to ponder the fates, he did now. Thinking of the years he'd spent at sea, fishing and lobstering, the catch and the haul. Sweat and toil went hand-in-hand with the brush of death that confronts a man daily when he sets out on a thirty-foot trawler to challenge the elements and harvest the sea of its life. He thought of that – life – the life he had made for himself and his wife Mildred, and the family they had raised. There, on the eastern frontier of Maine, on the shores of Bean's Point, in the Lost Kingdom of Moose Harbor. How fortunes here had risen and fallen with the rest of the country, if not the world, these past four years. The lobster catch had gone bust, but he had found a way to survive. He had always found a way to survive.

The shorter of the two men had walked up to him where he sat. The pistol was in his hand. He was sure the shorter man was going to pull the trigger without explanation. But then the taller one, who stood inside the parlor door, said, "I think you know why we're here, so I'll get to the point and we'll be off. Tell me, who have you been talking to?" He spoke softly, perhaps not wishing to disturb the other occupants in the house, all of whom were sleeping – or, more likely, to create an unnerving effect when he spoke. He had an accent; it was distinct and leant itself well to intimidation.

"Huh?" the man answered, utterly confused. "Who? About what?"

"I'll be more specific," the tall man said more forcefully. "Who did you speak with about your trip to Hyannis?"

The man in the chair thought about it for a moment, and then shook his head, "I don't know what you mean," he answered, barely above a whisper. "I've never set foot in Hyannis." He knew they wouldn't believe him anyway, but stalling meant surviving, he reasoned.

Survival, he had learned, and life, were a struggle. He had watched a man go under once, out to sea, while fishing. Though he had lunged to save him, the icy water sucked the man in when he fell, entangled within his own nets. The man was his grandfather and namesake, Minard, and he never came up. There was no time to say goodbye.

That was the first time he had seen someone die – but not the last. He had survived six grisly months in France over the spring and summer of 1918. Serving with the Twenty-Sixth, named the Yankee division because all the boys were from New England. The Yankees were sent to a remote hamlet, the Village of Seicheprey, to await orders. Nothing he had ever seen, heard of, or trained for could prepare him for what happened there that April day. How the German stormtroppers had descended on them, like winged demons, from the cover of *Foret de Mort Homme* – the Dead Man's Forest – took them all off guard. When they struck, the stormtroppers, he was with some boys from Connecticut, visiting a distant cousin, a fellow who shared the same last name as him, Severance. Anarchy and disarray erupted with the first shots. A friend of his from Moose Harbor, who was serving with him, shouted out the warning. It was enough for those who heard him to find cover, but not enough to save himself. Flamethrowing Huns immolated men to his left and to his right. The battle – the fight – was a brawl really, to the death. Fierce hand-to-hand combat up and down the narrow lanes and into the village square seemed to linger for hours. It was as though they were standing and fighting in the center of the Coliseum of ancient Rome, he imagined, not in the middle of some village in rural France, unknown to the world but forever branded into the body and soul of each and every man that made it out alive. There were no spectators in this coliseum, either. The villagers had fled in fear for their lives or burrowed deeply into their cellars in terror. They, the Yankees, were farmers and factory workers fighting battle-hardened gladiators. So desperate was the fight to survive, the cooks and the regiment's marching band joined the rumble. He watched one cook deflect bayonet thrusts with a skillet in one hand and hack two German soldiers to death with his meat cleaver in the other. Minutes later, he saw a stormtropper get brained with a tuba. The fight was a sad, tragic affair. Yet, when the day was done, somehow, he had survived.

The tall man, who had studied him for the past minute, sighed. "I don't believe you, but I would not expect anything less from you." The man was a Scot. Minard had met up with a regiment from the Highlands on his way to France. This one's eyes were as dark as his features. His brows were thick and wide and as heavy as the moustache that narrowed to the corners of his mouth. His square jaw was covered by a day's, perhaps two days', growth. The other man's face was covered by a heavy growth too. They had traveled a distance without stopping, like hunters, he reasoned, to find him. But why? For what?

These were hard men accustomed to leaving death in their wake, much like the stormtroppers at Seicheprey.

When he had made his way back home after the war, he thought all of that was behind him, the brutality of men – of humanity and its base predatory core – until now. The quiet safety of Moose Harbor was no more. There was the house fire which claimed the life of one of his mates. That left him unsure. He knew it was certain when they found his other mate drowned. An accident, they claimed, the risk a seafaring man takes, but Minard was wiser.

He found no solace that his children were mostly grown. They and Mildred were upstairs sleeping. If he shouted out or made a move in desperation, it would cost them their lives. Yet, he wanted to hold his wife one last time, look into her eyes, breathe in her essence, and say goodbye. He wanted to tell his children to make good with their lives, and above all, be happy. Minard knew, like his grandfather, there would be no time. All he could do was stare helplessly at the revolver in his face, make no sound, and hope none of them, his family, came downstairs.

"Do you know who I am?" the tall Scot asked.

Minard shook his head again, but said, without thinking, "One of the bad guys."

The Scot smiled. "That is relative to whose side one is on," he answered. "Or if one believes there are any sides at all."

"Who are you, then?" asked Minard.

"I am a messenger," the tall man replied, "and I have a message for you to deliver."

With those words, the man with the revolver lowered the pistol from Minard's face, then turned and stepped beside the tall Scot. Minard eased slightly in his chair. His bowels quaked. Beads of sweat, which had formed on his forehead and temples in those tense moments with the gun in his face, released, sliding down his face.

"Do you think you can deliver a message?" the Scot asked him.

"Yes," Minard said, and relaxed. He reached for his glass, and said, "May I?" The Scot nodded.

"It's an important message," the Scot said, "for the people you run for."

Minard swallowed some whiskey, and welcomed its burn. Somehow, he had survived, again, the brutality of men. When they left he would finish the bottle. "What do you want me to say to them?" he asked, and placed the tumbler down.

"It's not so much what I want to say to them, but the statement I wish to make to them," he replied.

"What might that statement be?" Minard asked, befuddled.

"Mr. Smith," the tall Scot addressed his companion. "Please convey to the man the statement we wish to send."

Minard looked at Mr. Smith, who stood to the right of the Scot, but Minard became momentarily distracted by a sudden burst of wind that struck the house, and a loud thunderclap that followed immediately. The vibration rattled the windows and made the house timbers creak and settle. In the distraction, he did not notice Mr. Smith raise his hand. Only when the lightning bolt struck and the second thunderclap exploded overhead did Minard notice Mr. Smith had his revolver aimed at him. He fired it as the thunder rolled – before Minard could react. The bullet struck him above his right eye and exited through the back of his skull into the fabric of the chair.

The paralytic grasp of his physical being was as instantaneous as the torturous pain. Slumped to the back and left corner of the chair, Minard felt the intense burn of the bullet's trajectory through his head. White hot needles, millions, singed the nerve endings of his brain along its path. He wanted to scream in agony as the scalding ice-pick sensation penetrated his skull and streamed through his body. But he could not move, motion, or scream.

His attention shifted from the pain and was drawn to the two men, where, for the first time, he noticed an inky, dark aura that seemed to envelope them. More alarmingly, even darker shadowy figures stood, or hovered actually, by them. Mr. Smith began to walk toward him, unencumbered by the darkness bound to his essence. Minard's first reaction was to jump at him, but as much as he willed himself to move, he could not. Mr. Smith placed the revolver in Minard's limp hand. Unexpectedly, one of the dark figures moved away from Mr. Smith's side and came closer to Minard. Eyes, set deep within its head, which Minard had not noticed before, began to smolder and glow like embers. The thing peered at him closely and sniffed several times. It appeared to smile, or at least Minard thought so at first, by the even darker, oily pitch of its mouth, which reeked of rot and waste. But then the thing's mouth continued to spread and open wider, forming a gaping hole, a dark, rancid pit, as though it was preparing to devour *him*. Minard distinctly heard a guttural, primordial growl bellow up from deep within the cavity, followed by another, and then several more. He was defenseless against the thing, and was struck by fear when realizing, in all probability, that he was looking into the abyss of hell itself, and he was seconds from being swallowed and cast into it.

But something happened. The air pressure around him shifted abruptly. The burn in his head began to recede, along with the pain. His thoughts drifted away from the hideous thing before him, and with it, all fear. In his mind's eye, his wife and children appeared, surrounding him, then his late parents, his siblings, his friends, and finally his grandfather. He saw his friend, too, the one who saved him in France. All of them crowded in around him. At the vision, the dark presence paused. Disappointed, angrily, its mouth closed slowly. Across the room a light flickered in midair, and from its center a vaporous purple haze began to sift through. It began to expand and billow and brighten. Mr. Smith turned and walked to the tall Scot, nodding, oblivious to the inky shadows and dark aura around them, and the increasing purple haze that spilled out and filled the room. The eyes of the thing in front of Minard dimmed, though. *It* could see the haze, and quickly it rushed to Mr. Smith's side, rejoining its host, finding its place among the other tarred demons.

The winged thing came from the ether, bursting into the room like a goddess affixed to the prow of a fleeting clipper ship. It was bathed in a radiant light, a violet hue, which filled the room with a warm glow. The thing wielded a scythe, too, that was starlit yet translucent. The gaze that fell upon Minard was one of angelic beauty, feminine and powerful. In her eyes he saw all there was and all he ever knew, but so much more. Through her eyes, he was sure, was immortal wisdom. "I am Markéta," she said, and then she swiped through some of the shadow figures with her scythe, leaving a swath of glistening amber stardust in its wake. That, and the inhuman squeal of the damned.

The winged thing reached Minard and took his hand. At the touch, a brilliant flash of violet burst through the room. The tall Scot and Mr. Smith could neither see Markéta nor the glow of purple haze that filled the parlor. The dark figures that clung to them, that she had not scythed, cowered at the flash and her presence, but the men, as men often do, remained indifferent to the light. What passed their eyes, a flash of lightning with a violet hue, went unnoticed.

"This is the end, then?" asked Minard, finally able to speak.

"No, old friend," Markéta answered.

Minard stood in spirit with the winged thing. Released from his body, he understood – became *aware* – as though he was and always had been – as though he had always known Markéta, who smiled, and then swung the blade of her scythe again, slicing open the fabric of time and space. Stars rippled and wobbled through matter. Purple light flowed out and a mass of energy, calm and peaceful, enveloped Minard. He drew on that energy, and that from within his very soul, and went with Markéta into the bliss.

The tall Scot and Mr. Smith went to the door. Quietly, they left the parlor without looking back at the body of Minard Severance. "Well stated," was all the Scot said to Mr. Smith, who acknowledged the remark with a nod as the pair left the house, fading into the night, like the roll of distant thunder.

Note from the Author

Acknowledgements, and how this book came about

In the winter of 2018, my publisher and editor, Jeffrey Zygmont, asked me if I had interest in writing a book of short stories, or maybe combining a few unpublished shorts with a collection of stories I had already published. I'm thinking, "Hell ya, baby!" but calmly replied, "Sure, sounds interesting." Even better, he said he wanted the collection of stories to be tilted toward tales of suspense and the supernatural with all of them taking place in Maine.

I wouldn't say I am uniquely qualified to write about Maine, but I do enjoying writing stories and I did grow up in the Woods of Maine. My family lived in a small town on the edge of the wilderness for 12 years. A town located in a county with more moose than people, a place that is still officially classified as the frontier. In recent years, I've gone back to spend good chunks of time there, finding inspiration to write.

Having agreed to put a collection of "wicked savage tales" together, we left the publication date open-ended. Me? I'm thinking I could pound out three or four stories by Halloween of 2018 and we'd be good to go. Ha! By Christmastime of 2019 I was still working on what, at that point, I was simply referring to as "the project," writing more stories than initially planned. That said, by then, we were closing in on a 2020 publication date, maybe spring, but no later than, say, Halloween.

And then 2020 happened. You didn't need to visit an eye doctor to see the reality of the world come into crystal clear focus. In comparison, when it came to publishing a collection of crazy, scary stories when every headline and lead story of every passing day was in itself a real-life, gut-wrenching crazy, scary story – without end – it just didn't seem right. So I asked the publisher, and he agreed, to put the book on hold until 2021.

Now, finally, 2021 has arrived and herein is a collection of ten stories for your reading entertainment. Though initial talk was for a collection that favored previously published material, in the end we included only four. Two Maine-related stories, "Howlin' Minnie" and "Reflections of Mr. Ivy" were from a previous collection, *Chill Your Cockles*, since out-of-print, and were in need of a new home. Another, "That Winged Thing," is a short story from *Tales From the moe.Republic,* that, we agreed, fit into this collection nicely.

The fourth previously published selection is the opening chapter from my 2017 supernatural suspense novel, *The Guardian Angel of Death*. We decided to include "Prelude to a Storm" here because it works as a freestanding story that nicely matches the "scary Maine" theme of the book. But it also is intended to serve as a teaser. While it stands on its own in this collection, you'll find the whole story that follows it in *The Guardian Angel of Death*.

The remaining six stories are new creations that have never seen a shade of ink.

To my family and friends who have put up with my rantings and writings over the years and, despite that, continue to welcome me into their homes, I thank you. And I thank Mr. Zygmont. First, as a publisher, for inspiring and publishing this collection of stories, and also his unwavering patience. Secondly, for his keen editing skills. He has truly taught me much over the years and, I feel, has made me a better writer for it.

Which brings me to the proverbial 'crux of the biscuit' and the heart of the matter: whether heading "upta" camp, a cottage down east, into the woods, the highlands, or spending a quiet night in town or down on the farm—wherever and however this book ends up in your hands—I can only hope, dear reader, that you take as much pleasure in reading these stories as I did in writing them.

John Derhak
Dover-Foxcroft
The Woods of Maine

www.ingramcontent.com/pod-product-compliance
Lightning Source LLC
Chambersburg PA
CBHW020130180626
46810CB00004B/1485